Katharine Haake's *What Happened Was* comes from a place of deep concern, for the climate, for our future, and for our passivity in times of crisis. These whimsical cautionary tales are written with a wry and unmistakable intelligence, and you can hear the echoes of outrage while feeling the power of human resilience.

—Leland Cheuk, author of *No Good Very Bad Asian*

PRAISE FOR HAAKE'S WORK

That Water, Those Rocks, is like a finely made watch with a transparent case that allows us to look inside and admire not only the beautiful ornamentation but the way it all works.

—*Los Angeles Times Book Review*

With the mesmerizing voice of a natural-born storyteller…Haake equates nature's basic elements (earth, fire, water) with those of mankind (love, livelihood, safety).

—*Booklist*

Original and accomplished…Haake's unusual narrative style is what truly sets this collection apart.

—*Kirkus*

Haake grew up in Northern California, and to judge by her new collection she may very well be the west coast's answer to the glittering stars of *New Yorker* heaven.

brary Journal

ically unspooling world. After each account I ended up feeling warm, giddy, very precarious, and hungry for more.

—Rod Val Moore, author of *Brittle Star* and *A History of Hands*

"Delight" is the wrong word for the experience of reading *What Happened Was*, so stuffed as it is with sorrow or loss or injustice, but Haake's control of her craft is profound. The emotional grip of these tales is firm and fast. Her sentences unroll with enormous facility and grace, and there is great comfort embedded in the telling, as if they are oral history, not fabulist prose. The accounts themselves are hardly comforting, of course. The reader believes they're enjoying words like yummy and braised and inky and xeriscaping but will read the final page with grief: The world is lost. The stories are over. This is the postworld.

—Katharine Coldiron, *Plan 9 from Outer Space* and *Junk Film*.

In Katharine Haake's astonishing "postworld" morality tales, narrators enumerate the earth's losses blithely, even at times comically, as their culpabilities add up. Here, ecological disintegration, "the raveling present," is a mere side-effect of human adaptation; Haake's characters admit their role in the destruction around them without ever losing buoyant faith in the choices that lead them there. Haake's light touch and shining prose render *What Happened Was* all the more devastating.

—Dorothy Barresi, author of *American Fanatics* and *Rouge Pulp*

What Happened Was

Katharine Haake

Requests for permission should be directed to 1111@1111press.com, or mailed to 11:11 Press LLC, 4732 13th Ave S, Minneapolis, MN 55407.

Book Design by Mike Corrao
Cover Design by Matthew Revert
Cover Art by Lisa Bloomfield

Paperback: 9781948687667

Printed in the United States of America

FIRST AMERICAN EDITION

9 8 7 6 5 4 3 2 1

for Arden, and all the others just starting out

A body is a body, but only voices are
capable of love.

—Ricardo Piglia

CONTENTS

Prolog

After a while it started to seem that this was the way things had always been.

Every morning, we woke up in our same bed, our same disaster looming over us, same as the day before and the next day coming up. Had there ever been a time our disaster hadn't loomed? We ate our eggs and drank our milk. These were the things we had always done. But weren't the sunny centers of our eggs a little less golden these days; wasn't the milk a tad turned? And didn't they taste of chemicals?

Not that we hadn't seen our disaster barreling down on us. Everybody knew it was coming. But we didn't take much notice right at first—who'd ever have believed such a thing?

We should have known, of course. Things seemed pretty good back then, but they weren't going to stay that way forever. You couldn't stop it; I couldn't stop it. None of us could.

Later, some of us felt all sucker-punched-thrown-for-a-loop, but others, pretty much *whoop-dee-doo*, as if they'd been hoping for something like this all along and now it was here. The way they looked at things was us-vs-them. We just never noticed before.

But I knew a disaster when I saw it.

First, the edges of everything—it's hard to know quite how to say this—*frayed*.

The sky had a tinge of the dun.

Then, *wham*, fire, fire everywhere. Or else water, water.

Soon everything tasted of chemicals.

One day, a bunch of them came to my door and, in their eyes, something haunted—or hunted. Haunted and hunted are almost the same, only one letter is different. Each of them carried a thing in their hands. It wasn't a weapon, per se. But it wasn't a not weapon either. They could use it for their protest as well as to protect them, also one letter off.

I knew they were there. I knew what they wanted.

But there's a big difference between being in the thrall of a disaster and being in its maw.

They weren't the last—there were going to be more. But a chemical taste in my eggs wasn't the worst that could happen. All in all, the sky was blue enough for now.

I'm not saying I was right or wrong in what I did or didn't do. My door was my temple is what I thought then. Nothing got through my door that I didn't let in.

Looking back, it's clear as day we brought our disaster on ourselves. Despite our cheerful nature and our firm belief in progress, we'd been rushing headlong toward it all along.

Well, everyone said, what happened, happened. At least we said, it didn't happen here.

But that's where we were wrong: Of course, it did.

Here's where it happened the most.

Part 1

Emissaries From the Postworld

Why shouldn't we—men, gods, and world—
be someone's dreams, someone's thoughts,
marooned forever outside existence?

—Fernando Pessoa

Account A

The aliens were neither curious nor vicious, but they were hungry—monstrously so. In truth, the persistence of their eating was like nothing we had ever seen before. They ate and ate. And yet, we felt no judgment, for it was clear to us that they were neither gluttonous nor greedy but merely famished, as if they had traveled a vast distance and arrived at our woods in a state of such depletion that their eating would go on and on forever. While we, a gentle, hospitable people, did our best to feed them.

But it was hard.

They were, by all appearances, insatiable, consumed by a strangely mechanical appetite that belied both preference and habit. Whatever we placed before them they ingested with the same systematic resolve that evinced neither pleasure nor distaste. And what we placed before them was a lot.

One apparent youth—a female, we surmised from her slightly smaller size and round physique—fed so insistently we could not help but speculate as to her condition. While the others could devour vast quantities of wheat or cabbage before collapsing all at once into large, lethargic lumps, her cravings, in some ways more meticulous, were also more relentless. She took small helpings and did not gorge on seconds, but neither did she ever stop to rest. I once watched her myself as she swallowed two hand mirrors whole, a bloated container of dewy mown hay, and my last pair of shoes in a single meal, saving the laces for last and sucking them up with a satisfied slurp that was almost pleasant if not for my having to go barefoot in the days ahead.

In all other respects, they were the mildest of guests—easygoing, unassuming, and distinguished by a gentle, undifferentiated oral morphology—low, mellifluous purring punctuated with the occasional bark, cluck, or coo—that we found to be oddly consistent with the overall amorphousness of form and faintly rancid smell they'd arrived with, wafting out of nowhere on a sour breath of wind one morning as we rose from our sleep. We looked out and there they were adrift in our fields, although with no apparent means of locomotion (lacking even discernible limbs), they seemed somehow to hover a mere hair above the earth.

Naturally we welcomed them—these aliens, *our* aliens—openhearted and ebullient. It had been so long since anything new had happened to us, just seeing them there lifted something in our spirit we hadn't even known was low.

But what to do, how to show them *mi casa es su casa,* come in, sit down, kick back, put your feet up (if they had feet)? And because they seemed neither to need nor even to desire physical shelter, we sometimes felt as if they must prefer to sleep upon the rocky ground beneath the starry sky despite the various comforts of our homes, which we would no more have denied them than the last sweet yellow onions or delicate preserves from our musty root cellars, our few remaining bottles of ritual wine.

We fed them instead. We spent whole days laboring over our most prized delicacies—smoked oysters and aromatic artichokes, subtly spiced purees of apricots and stews of sassafras and rutabaga, daily breads so light they sometimes rose from their pans and squished on our ceilings with fragrant emissions, quail egg omelets, truffle soufflés. Then we laid them out—tremendous feasts—on our windowsills or stoops, the enormous serving bowls steaming in the morning air. But the aliens weren't picky, and as they seemed to take as much gustatory pleasure in our thorny bushes and moldy grass clippings as they did in our freshest vegetables and most succulent fruits, by and by, we abandoned our cooking.

And just in the nick of time, there being little left to cook.

Still, they had to eat, and eat they did.

After our shoes, the bedding went next, leaving us almost giddy with delight as we stripped our mattresses and tossed our linens out to them, for sheets were largely troublesome, their laundry a disagreeable chore.

Take that, we exclaimed. They're full of starch. And isn't starch salty—or sweet?

The coverlets went next, fluffed and fragrant with feathers, their quills a delectable crunch. Finally, our pillows, stuffed with new down and years of dead skin, until at last we found ourselves huddled fully clothed three or four to a bed, spooned like spent lovers and shivering like boys at play in the field.

And although it would not be long before they were eating the rest of our world, it was the younger, smaller female who dove in first, beginning on the fences we had built over many generations. How ravenous she seemed now, how utterly insatiable, nibbling her way through our rails and posts until all that had once served to separate the land of one neighbor from the land of another disappeared down her alien gullet. The paving stones went next, popping out with little suction sounds from where they had lain throughout the span of our collective memories like something pried loose and released. And as the aliens continued to strip our built world bare, the sound of their chewing turned sonorous and deafening; their terrible digestive rumblings filled our long nights.

Yet there was something pleasing, too, about those hours, for as we lay together, bare of foot and bedding, our bodies sought the bodies of others, interlacing our various parts in the coldest hours between three and six in the morning. We woke blushing, but slept better, our limbs looser, less constrained in the open air.

But it was not until the younger, smaller female with the rapacious appetite began nibbling at the roofs of our houses that we saw—truly *saw*—how it was going to be. The night sky thus revealed as a dazzling quilt of dreams, we wrapped ourselves beneath it, sharing even that (for what else did we have?), and turned in tangled rapture toward our bedmates.

When the last home was razed and we stood naked in the dawn, facing one another as we never had before, we saw reflected in our neighbors the shocked determination not to be afraid, even as the younger, smaller female was already swooping down upon the smallest among us, a child still wet from the womb. Despite what we had seen of their hunger, not one of us moved to stop what happened next.

Without arms to take the infant, the alien stooped, bending close above to inspect it while the mother of this new suckling child—as if in this they shared a common bond—turned her soft maternal gaze upon the huddled thing. We were all watching as she seemed to hesitate, but only briefly. And then she did what any one of us would do—she held the child out. She cooed to it to soothe it, but she held it out.

When the younger, smaller female alien was satisfied, she made a clucking sound. Then all at once, a tremendous cacophony as, alien by alien, they stooped to examine the rest of us who, caught up in the headiness of the moment, could not quite take in their proximity, no more than we could yet anticipate the loneliness that was coming just ahead when the aliens would leave us. The way we liked to tell it was how gladly we'd have offered ourselves to them!

If only we had buttered up! But with what butter?

In this way, alone among ourselves—a gentle, hospitable people—and with the dead of winter coming on, we took tenderly to feeding one another once again.

Account K

A man awakened with a knot in his side.

All blasé about it, his wife brought him coffee, as usual, and for a treat, a big bowl of berries and milk.

Shorts too snug? she said, gobbling up the berries for herself. Breathe deep and rub it gently. There now, feel better?

But the man did not feel bad, only confused. Why him? He was just an ordinary man, with ordinary hopes and dreams, like anybody else, but there was nothing normal about his condition. The knot wasn't hard—more like pressure than a pain—but it was unquestionably present and would persist, he felt certain, as a part of him forever. Soon he would have to name it, this peculiar thing inside him, all new, not him—separate from him—and strangely vibrant, almost alive.

That night, the man's wife braised lamb and artichokes, their tender leaves opening suggestively at the heart, but distracted, the man hardly touched his food.

Where was he supposed to put it anyway, with the

knot taking up so much room inside him?

Yummm, the man's wife said, isn't this tasty! Isn't this good!

The next day, the same, and the day after that.

Of course, he had known all along that something like this was going to happen, but now that it had, he didn't know quite what to feel, couldn't altogether account for the awfulness of it, the persistent shame of his own private being, as if everything he'd always believed about himself had suddenly taken a powerful, inexplicable twist. He was he, and then, all at once, he was he-plus-not-he, utterly transfigured by a presence no one else would ever fathom.

But time is a powerful healer, and it wasn't long before the knot—the pressure, the alive thing inside him—began to feel familiar, even reassuring, the way, when he breathed, the air slid to its side, his lungs adjusting to accommodate it; the way, when he slept, it shifted his dreams one dream over, as if he were dreaming the wrong dream, the one that belonged to the night before or the night after, or even to the woman sleeping stolidly beside him. The man could make love only from one side now. If he tried to sing, the notes came out high or low.

Still, the man's wife continued to serve the most succulent meats and freshest fruits for the meals he continued to pick at. She offered him her body, warm and unambivalent, but more and more he found himself turning, instead, to the knot.

Anyone could see this was impossible, yet would go on forever.

Anyone could see the wife was losing patience, like anyone would.

Soon she began to nag.

See someone, she said. Call a doctor.

Not hungry? she said, more for me. But the wife was putting on weight, and she sounded resentful.

Then she whined. I'm your wife—I want all of you. Please, she said, where does it hurt?

But of course, it didn't hurt, so what was there to say?

The knot, which at first had seemed amorphous, had begun to assume something like a shape, oblong and curved, like an egg, and with a different temperature, a degree or two above or below his own, nestled near his heart like a secret or a promise. But of what—was there something lacking in his life, something primal or essential? Was he about to find out?

Thus, it was inevitable that the man began to regret ever having mentioned it at all, for his wife could never let it go now, nor ever understand. And so, he had no choice but to gather himself possessively around it, turning ever more hurtfully away from the woman who had been, until now, his lifelong lover and companion. In bed, he'd roll his back to her, curled on his good side, and when he was certain she was asleep, her breathing deep and steady and filling both sides of her strong, symmetrical lungs, he'd stroke the place on his side where the knot was, gently, soothingly, as though, if he were only attentive enough, it would reveal itself to him in such a way that they could be together for all the world to see.

The man so believed in the inevitability of this union that he began to lose sleep, stroking and stroking his knot the night through, his stomach empty and growling as he grew lean and lightheaded with longing.

Then one night, as inexplicably as it had first appeared, the knot left him.

At first, when he woke, all he felt was a strange sense of disorientation, the different parts of his body completely at odds, leaving him panting and profoundly irritated with his still sleeping wife, who smiled gently at him from some distant dream that belonged precisely and entirely to that moment. Then slowly, very slowly, he began to be aware of his internal organs shifting, one by one, back into the empty spaces left open by the absent knot, ruthlessly returning to their anatomically correct positions with the heaviness of lead.

And *oh!* that did hurt. That—not the knot, but the knot's absence—was the true meaning of pain, which left the man, raging and bereft, in a state of deep despair. Beside him, the woman—his wife—lay a stranger to him now, and although he'd have given anything to reach out and touch her if he'd had any hope of arresting the relentlessness of lack going on inside his body, his hand sought instead the blank spot on his side where the knot used to be and where a strange coolness, like death, was already settling.

Account G

In the end, the woman might almost have been expecting the tear—or *rip*—that appeared with no warning in the sky one day.

But of course, the woman was a mother, no stranger to dread. Strongest in the milky light of dawn as she struggled from her sleep, it waxed and waned around such daily troubles as another child's snubbing of her son, their mounting bills, the current war, and coming end of days. And while the woman's dread could be said to be among the most acute and persistent of her feelings—part and parcel of the full range of human experience—mainly she longed to be normal, like everyone else.

The tear, though, that was real. It wasn't big, hardly more than the miniscule fray, a queer anomaly. Time to get your eyes checked, the woman told herself, probably a floater, thinking of all the other terrible things it could also be—Fuchs dystrophy, macular degeneration, retinal detachment, impending blindness. The woman imagined her dotage, groping around in her little house as if for some sign of her son. But no, it was a tear all right—half the length of an infant's thumb not far above the lemon tree outside her bedroom window.

By day, it hung there darker than the darkest dread—darker than obsidian or coal or deep inside a cave. And by night, the opposite, a blinding dash of light, as if another sun were blasting from behind. The only other thing, the woman soon discovered, was how it could affect the weather underneath, a breath of cool breeze on a sweltering day, a bead of heat on a cold one.

Of all the things to happen, the woman thought. What if it expanded, growing over time into a massive black hole that sucked in Earth itself, or blew up into a radiant star, or fell like a meteor—them and the dinosaurs—*phlaaapth*. Why her? the woman thought. What did she need with another worry? She already had worries galore.

For example, her son's second-grade teacher, with whom the already too sensitive boy spent so much of these, his impressionable years, was an ill-tempered crank without an ounce of human kindness to her nature, and if you weren't one of her pets, she'd turn on you in the front of the class and tear up your homework—*rip, rip, rip*—for everyone to see. The woman had seen it herself, the poor reviled object of the teacher's scorn—*you stupid, careless boy!*—slumped over in a huddled clump of shame. Of course, that particular child was among the more hapless of those bussed in from another part of town, so maybe some carelessness had been involved. But when it happened to the woman's son (who was also careless), *oh, oh!* How could she possibly endure it?

Still, a transfer to another class was out of the question because all the other mothers thought the teacher had high academic standards and also because of the goats. Not fish or guinea pigs or sweet-tempered budgies, the woman thought with some chagrin, but goats—one spotted and one white one, with little goat hooves and plaintive goat bleats—the rangy pair of which would go home for the weekend with the lucky boy or girl named Master of Goats. Every child got their chance—that was both a promise and a rule. So when the teacher posted monitors for the coming week at the end of school on Thursday, while most of the kids had to clean the erasers or empty the trash or put away books, one got to sweep out the dung in the yard and feed the goats hay from the barrel.

Naturally, the boy loved the goats. He loved everything about them—their soft goat hair and gangly legginess, their grassy smell, their pointy ears and twitchy snouts and ruminating cud. Most of all, he loved the sadness of their oblong eyes, their black, rectangular pupils reminding the woman of nothing so much as her worrisome tear. But the boy loved the goats and the woman loved the boy, so when he'd wake up Thursday morning in a frenzy of excitement and anxiety (*it's going to be me!/ what if it's not me?*) she could not help but keep her fingers crossed while, apart from her, the boy spent the long hours of his schoolday tied up in knots about who it would be. All that waiting forged a common bond among the children if not so much the parents, especially the woman, who wasn't sure she wanted the goats. Goats were browsers, she had learned, and while her backyard wasn't much, she hated to think how much less it was going to be once they'd had their way with it. But if you were a parent, you did your part. You borrowed someone's minivan or asked the gardener for a favor or figured out some other way to get the goats home where you made them welcome from the close of school on Friday to its start on Monday, feeding them kibble and table scraps, the occasional family rosebush, and all the begonias.

So, while this too filled the woman with dread, the boy lived for nothing but his turn as Master of Goats. All week, he'd be dreaming his dreams of nuzzling the goats all weekend, counting the days until Thursday. But as the year dragged on and his name was never called, he began to develop the same little slump to his shoulders that afflicted the bussed-in child and that, like the tear in the fabric of the universe, only the woman could see. Even at the time, she knew she should say something, step up and tell the teacher not to overlook her son who, in addition to his carelessness, could be a little restive. How hard would that have been? She could at least have sent a note: It's our turn now—we want the goats!

Although, in truth, she did not.

When the final Thursday came, the boy leapt from his bed and cried out from the tail end of sleep, oh, happy day—my turn at last! And Mom, she saved me for the three-day weekend!

But no. The teacher looked right at him and then called the name of a girl—a sweet, little pixie with a room mother mom and a tractable nature to match her blond curls—who'd already had the goats all winter break.

When the woman picked the boy up after school, she saw the slight at once in his more slumped shoulders and the new, crushed squint in his teary left eye that caused a rush of her own grief to well up inside her and inspired a halfhearted trip for ice cream. And her pain was nothing compared to her son's, which surely would linger as he grew.

It lingered. More in her, it sometimes seemed, than in him, where it was hard to distinguish from other telltale signs of childhood anxiety—tics, sleep disturbances, an air of melancholy between bouts of bad behavior.

In later years, the woman could not always remember if the tear had appeared before or after the girl who'd already had her turn got the goats a second time, but it confirmed that the internal dread she'd harbored for so long had its true origin elsewhere, as if ubiquitous to the structure of the universe itself in a vindication so profound she could not but accept it the same way she'd accepted the cruelty of other children and teachers. From that one torn spot, the woman surmised many things: War was coming, wild tigers would soon be extinct, the American West (where the woman made her home) would go down to drought and conflagration, the small nest egg she'd accrued for rainy days or retirement would be depleted by crises in the market she could never understand, tyrants would rule.

Her son would grow up. He would forget her birthday.

The woman would die.

But then a strange thing happened.

As, one by one, all these things came to pass, the tear—or *rip*—in the sky continued to shed its different temperature down on the lemon tree where, if the woman stood awash in it, things didn't seem so bad.

Oh, the war. Well, war was a terrible thing. Everyone knew that. But all wars eventually came to their end.

Losing the tigers, now that was sadder, but the absence of tigers caused the memory—or idea—of them to become so deeply cherished that people all over the world resolved to be better stewards of the planet and its remaining animals.

Drought inspired xeriscaping, the beautiful recovery of deserts, and a more resourceful people who better lived within their means.

Her son did grow up, and he did forget her birthday; indeed, it often seemed that he'd forgotten her entirely. But by then, birthdays no longer seemed important.

In this way, as the woman moved into her dotage, despite its aches and pains, she grew to cherish the tear—or *rip*—which over the years had eased her trepidation in so many little ways, altering her essential disposition to embrace this new, peculiar vein of optimism. It was true: The world was a dreadful place, full of human misery and woe. But even long before the goats, the woman always knew the end was coming. Between now and when it did, if there was a human condition, let it be a condition of hope!

Of course, it's possible she was growing a bit feeble in her mind. She was no longer young. The death she had foreseen would soon be upon her.

One day, not her birthday, the woman's son—a fine young man with beautiful teeth and an easy manner, a stranger to her now—came bearing flowers for no reason on earth. And seeing him walking toward her, the woman was flooded with such a tremendous sense of relief and love that she hardly noticed the small tear—or *rip*—forming just above his left eye and from which another temperature was coming.

Account E

Despite our better judgment, we were watching the television news when the event occurred, and so we nearly missed it altogether. We knew we really shouldn't, but we couldn't stop ourselves. All around the world, such goings on—you can't imagine—and with people far and near proving either savage or heroic, we couldn't tear our eyes away, even as our children ran about unsupervised, without shoes, their homework undone.

Later, we'd remember everything differently. It started with a color, one of us insisted, a tinge of ochre in the sky. But no, another said, I heard a bang. And so forth, until our words trailed off into a quiet dolor and no one had any words left for what had happened to us.

Then the child spoke. He spoke, as children do, in a high, sweet voice with a bit of a lisp, the words spilling out all at once.

The darkness, he said, came on with no warning. We were outside in the green trees—couldn't you *hear* us? We could hear you on the inside, listening to your television news. But how were we supposed to get back to you now?

Of course, we hadn't heard them. Somewhere, storms were howling, wildfires spreading. Don't breathe—the air will kill you. War raged.

And get down, the child continued, to what? When we saw what we saw, we all shrieked together, a singular howl. Surely, you must have heard that!

But no, the first we noticed was when we called the children in for dinner. Not right away (high up in the government men were having sex with women not their wives), but when the children didn't come, when their dinners had gone cold (seas and coups were rising, toxic plumes and global plagues) we shouted out to them the terrible things we saw happening on TV.

If you don't come in now, we'll send you to bed without any supper. We waited a bit before issuing our sternest of threats: We'll make you watch the television news with us, and then you will know how lucky you are.

Now the child spoke again in his high, sweet way: We heard you calling and wanted to come in—we wanted to be good! But how could we get down with nothing to get down to? The trees were still there and the houses with you inside calling for us, but everything in between—the earth itself and the rocky ground that once had held the houses and the dear little path we walked on to get to the trees—gone! It glistened, the child explained, as if we hadn't been there too. But that's all, only the glistening, and when one of us climbed down to test it, watch out! That's when we knew the real trouble we were in.

On the inside, finally, we heard it—the gurgling slurp of that first little child going down and the final muted *pop* like a fragile bubble bursting: *pop, pop, pop!* One child down, the others in the trees, and all those TV dinners going cold.

But who could miss that furtive, little *pop?*

For once, we turned our televisions off to consider what was happening just outside, our own children trapped in the green trees over there and all that nothing in between. After the first rush of panic, a kind of dispassionate logic prevailed—they were our children, after all. Our first duty was to nurture and protect them. One of us, holding an orange and not really thinking (for where would we get another orange now?), tossed it out toward the children huddled without supper in the trees, but *plop*, it fell short to the nothing below where *pop*, it was gone like the boy.

At that, our mouths filled up with saliva and a terrible craving for oranges.

The next thing we heard were the cries of our children, who had also seen the orange disappear.

One of the smallest fell that night. The popping was quieter—she was so tiny—but we all heard it anyway for none of us could sleep. And *oh!* we rued the carelessness with which we'd let them roam. If only we had made them do their homework; if at least we had made them wear shoes. In shoes, could they have walked across the nothing back to us? If they were doing homework, they would not have been out climbing trees.

In the morning, they were hungry and cranky. We knew we had to feed them, but how to feed them now?

Someone turned the television news on to drown out the sounds of their whining, but no calamity on earth could compare now to our own. So we put our heads together and chipped in this or that—some nuts and bolts and cogs and gears, a cable of this and a bucket of that, and baskets of hardboiled eggs—and then we rigged a pulley system out of everything we had to send our children wholesome snacks and other consolations—blankies and booties to ward off the chill, picture books and yoyos to stave off the doldrums, animal plush toys to fill up their small, lonesome arms. And after that, we somehow adapted to the plight of our children stranded in the trees and us in our houses, apart from them.

From what we saw on the television news, we knew the kind of hardship people could endure—who were we to think we were so special? Buck up, we told one another, steeling ourselves to our empty arms and the occasional plop of the children falling like leaves from the trees. It still tore at our heartstrings, of course (whose child was that?), but we tried not to let it get our spirits down.

When the last child, but one, was gone, with no one left to play with and no hope of being rescued, the one remaining boy—who stood before us now—added up the pros and cons, thought about his TV dinners and snug trundle bed at home, and surveyed the subtle glistening one last time. Then he hoisted his lithe, little body into the bucket and slid himself back to us.

It was easy, he said, in his high, sweet voice and lisping lilt.

He wasn't very big, but he was strong, and as we considered him there on the porch he seemed as childlike as ever but, we saw now, all alone on this earth. It was this—his aloneness—that forced us finally to take in the event, not just what had happened to the very ground that once had lain between us in our homes and our children in their trees, but also each of the soft, sucking slurps that had marked a boy or girl disappearing.

My, how you've grown, one of us said as another bent to sniff the child's hair and still another scooped him to her lap, tickling the cleft of his delicate chin and kissing the down on the nape of his neck.

I stood in the doorway looking out at the green trees glowing in the dying sun, the dark expanse of earth now restored between us. The child who had spoken—our last and only one—slipped off the lap he'd been clutched on and sidled slyly up to me, nudging his small, soft hand into mine like a furtive animal or tiny, beating heart. We stood there for a moment, listening to the sound of the television news.

Then the child tugged as if to lead me down the path. And while I thought what he was saying was *let me show you where they went*, I heard something else ahead, but for the life of me I cannot tell you what it was.

Account F

One day a flower appeared where nothing ever was before. It had been so long since any one of us had seen such a thing, we weren't sure what to call it at first.

Um, one said.

A-hem, another said.

Until one of us arrived at the word: flower.

It's a *flower*, she said, the italics all hers, as if otherwise it might have been a railroad or rhinoceros. Words like that didn't slide off the tongue anymore, not like fortitude and perseverance, not like grit. There was something so provocative and, in other ways, unmitigated about this flower—its bright yellow petals speckled with blue and veined with filaments of umber and a shade of paint we once called elephant—we found ourselves entranced.

Well, that's how it was right there at the start.

The petals, which were large and ovular, had a kind of fuzz that rippled in the breeze, as if alive.

Of course, it's alive, we said. It's a *flower*.

We thought about this for a while, but what no one said was, like *before*, because what was so great about before anyway? Well, besides railroads and rhinoceroses, besides flowers.

And so we took to chatting amiably about it as we waited in our queues, each with a theory as to what it might portend—an end to strife, more of everything, rain. Some made cheerful wagers on when it might be joined by another. Others took to having little gatherings around it. You couldn't really call them parties because not even the lighthearted among us indulged in such frivolity as that, but at four o'clock each afternoon, people gathered at the site bearing bottles of whatever they had left to drink and bags of their last remaining snacks to savor with the others as they visited together and reveled in the flower.

In all its speckled comeliness, one said.

Or fragrant bouquet, another offered, although this gave us pause. Did it even have an odor? It was hard to tell. Weren't flowers supposed to smell sweet?

Like honey, one blithely remarked, for most of us remembered honey.

No, no, another said. Like honeysuckle!

Ha, another said, honeysuckle *is* a flower. You can't say that—a flower is a flower.

Then one of the least favored among us used a word we'd all forgotten. That, she said, is a *tautology*. She said it quietly but with the air of smug superiority we all disliked in her. Who used words like that anymore, words loaded with privilege?

Being the type to keep to myself, I wasn't there, of course, but I *heard* about it. We all did. News of that word spread like what we once called wildfire. Still, we tried not to judge her despite what she thought of us. The flower had appeared. It was speckled and had a scent we found hard to describe—maybe bristly? That's what we knew. That's all we wanted to know.

Most of us had some books at home, but we didn't read them. What for? They were still useful as doorstops, or stepstools or the occasional barricade, and if you had enough of them to pile into an ottoman, you could put your feet up and kick back without anything taxing about it. So it is perhaps for this reason that none of us—neither the lighthearted nor the somber among us—were expecting it when the one who used words to flaunt herself above the rest of us appeared at the side of the flower one day with a book—a very large book, what we once called a tome.

Well, as soon as we heard about this, we all went there at once, even the very old, even the children—even me. When we arrived, she was already at it, the book opened out like a flower of its own beside the flower that was growing from the very ground we stood on and where she herself was kneeling with a mien of such fierce concentration that, by comparison, we were made to feel petulant and small. For there before us on the pages of the book were not words, but drawings—bright and colorful drawings of so many different flowers you could never believe them all!

The girl, on her knees, had a pinched crease in the bridge above her nose.

Harrumph, one said, bending in close to see.

But the girl kept intently turning pages as if she was thinking of something not us, maybe searching for a word, or a genus or a genome for this flower that had appeared where nothing was before. We thought about that nothingness and couldn't stop the feeling that began to run among us, a kind of wonder: For how could it be possible that the world—*our* world—had once contained such flora, each plant so extravagant in color and form?

Such bounty, one of us marveled at last.

Ah, I sighed, yes—such *surfeit*.

Account F2

You wouldn't have thought we could keep it up for as long as we did, despite our being young and full of vigor. But the vast schools of small golden fish had appeared out of nowhere, and who knew when they would disappear again? Like smelt, they ran up our shores in the inky dark of the predawn chill where we, who went to revel in their glut, took to scooping them up in our satchels and shoes, their scales rubbing off until we too were glowing with them. Then we raised our faces to the moon and howled. We turned to admire each other, all slimy and golden: Oh, weren't we beautiful, weren't we fine!

We knew the rules, of course. We weren't supposed to be out near the water after dark or ever let our feelings show, but *oh, oh, oh*! Once we got started, just look at everything that was coming out now. It turned out you could eat them, lick the scales raw off your fingers or the backs of your classmates standing knee-deep beside you in the shimmering pulse of the gentle waves that brought the fish in and then took them away. And they were so very delicious. They gave us what we only knew to call a special feeling, like an energy, but energy is not what it was. It was like love, but not love—not like anything we already knew. We only knew it by what it was not.

So that's how it started, the hoarding, one golden scale at a time. We peeled them, scale by scale, fish by fish, stashing our loot in secret jars with a little extra stuffed in our pockets so as always to have some to suck after gym or before a big test. The color of the fish was more yellow than gold, but the deeper down you peeled, the more brightly it gleamed, until we began to suspect that at the center of the fish lay not heart or gut but tiny nuggets of pure gold bullion.

Gluttony did not become us, but our want was our want.

Of course, we knew the trouble we'd be in if anybody knew, but we couldn't stop ourselves. We sneaked out for our romps and came home with our jars to hide under piles of our rumpled clothes or behind stacks of our child-hood books. We did this every night, slipping back to our beds before dawn, all sated and replete.

But even then we knew it could not last forever.

And so, it wasn't long before our festive feelings faded, giving way to a pensive somberness that now marked our nightly visitations with the fish. Maybe not all at once, but little by little, we stopped howling like dogs at the moon and slipped into a kind of muted reverence instead.

There wasn't much left in the ocean anymore, not much alive. That it had yielded up such bounty to us astonished and humbled us both. We meant to do right by those fish who'd come, we saw now, to teach us that, despite our current troubles, we should get good grades in school, eat less and exercise more. For a harvest was a harvest even so, and maybe these fish—our own golden fish—were the last of their kind, and maybe we were too.

We went in the night to stand with the fish—emissaries from the darkest depths of the dying seas—and we couldn't stop fierce affections from surging among us. At home, alone in our bedrooms, our jars of golden scales threatened daily to expose us, but here among the others, we faced each other openly as if, whatever was going to happen, we would meet it together.

You weren't supposed to hurt the fish; you were just supposed to peel them gently and then let them go. Everybody knew this: catch and release, right was right.

But the backs of the fish had a little plume of frill, and we found we could pet them like pets (when there were pets). Petting the fish gave us another kind of feeling from our first heady peeling, and once we got started—stroking and stroking the feathery quills flat to the muscular bodies—everything settled into stillness, and it was just you and the fish then, the fish quivering in your hand and you gazing down into its one facing-up eye. All around, others would be stroking their own fish—everyone side-by-side in the waves, bathed with milky moonlight and staring down into their fish's eyes.

We weren't around when the oceans started dying, but we knew a miracle when we saw it. Dead herrings (when there were herrings) phosphoresced.

If our fish were to die, what might they *do*?

Well, sure, we saw plenty of dead ones because, the same as with smelt (when there were smelt), the tide brought the fish in and it took them away, but sometimes it left some behind. Those left-behind fish on the beach, we couldn't let them go to waste—of course not! A harvest was a harvest even so.

No one knows who was the first one to do it, but one of us discovered if you petted hard enough—really dug in—beneath the top glittery layer of scale there was a stubborn membrane that clung toughly to the fish like a plate of body armor or a vital organ. But you could get it off. It maybe took a little force, but you did it anyway because underneath the skin, a kind of milky flesh, and underneath that, the secret, inner parts. You had to use your fingernails or shards of ancient shells to claw your way into your dead, beached fish, and when you were done, you tossed whatever was left back into the water, little gutted lumps of entrails and heads bobbing about in the froth of the waves that lapped at our knees.

I'm not saying we were right or wrong in anything we did. Despite our frolicking, we knew times were hard. We knew this from the fretting of our parents, but also from the whining of our siblings, the littlest ones who were starting to waste. Who wouldn't crave the taste of the meat? It wasn't sweet and it wasn't not not sweet: It was protein.

We went in the night to commune with the fish, and if one of the ones that was already dead gave up its good parts that found their way into your pocket, who could hold it against you? If you fed it to your sister, or secretly ate it yourself under your covers alone in your bed, who was going to tell? And if one day you did to an alive and thrashing fish what you'd already done to a dead one from the beach—if you dug into its insides for its secret layers and parts, if you *hurt* it—who would stop you?

Not any one of us, that was for sure. We were going to go to stand with the fish for as long as we could, and when we couldn't do that anymore, we were going to do what anyone would do.

Account N

A child came into the world missing a part although in other respects she was perfect, and the curve of the nub where her part should have been, serene as the arc of an egg or a moon, would prove, in the end, to be functional, if clumsy. But that's not why people loved her; people loved her, despite her deficiency, because she was gentle, and she was kind, and she was good.

We knew the rules of course, it being forbidden to harbor anomalies, and while some (like this child's) were innate, others took time to develop and were subtle, or they came on all at once with no warning.

My own father's face did not begin to blur until I was in grade school, and even then, the progression was slow. Most of the time he at least looked familiar, but then, in vague ways, he did not.

This went on for several years, and throughout the time it took for his features to lose their once distinctive qualities—the bridge of his nose becoming indistinguishable from his inner arc of brow, his lips smearing into his chin, the strong line of his jaw drooping into his jowl—we could almost ignore it. Whereas, with the family down the street, it happened all at once. They went to bed one night and woke up the next morning to find the mother rendered monstrous overnight.

These things happened.

Farther south, in the larger towns and cities where things were more developed, it never would have happened the way it happened here, so it was not without some apprehension that we let the girl grow.

It's a slippery slope, my father harangued, as if he were not already on it.

After he was gone and the mother down the street, our two families merged, siblings grinning awkwardly across the supper table at other siblings not our own, the new replacement parent not quite fitting into the space where the other, prior parent once had sat. It wasn't the same, but it was all right. Everyone tried to make do. The rules were clear.

But with the girl, for some reason, we overlooked the most fundamental of them and did not avert our eyes but longed, instead, to take in every bit of her—up to and including her absent part. Such unorthodox behavior was not without its consequence, and as word of it could not get out, we let ourselves be cut off from the larger towns and cities to the south and severed ties with distant relatives for her and our protection.

Ah, but wasn't she pretty, wasn't she fine?

Just looking at her made us feel fine too. What need had we of others when we had her; what need had she for her absent part when she had us? That was the way it all made sense.

All in all, it's safe to say I loved her best, for it was I who chose her first when we were picking teams or partners for school projects and who affected both her manner and her dress. We shared the same seat on the bus each day, spent every lunch hour and recess together, and had regular after school playdates. And on weekend sleepovers in the dead of night when everyone else was fast asleep, we'd slip naked from the sheets to dance in the milkiest light of the moon, commingling all of our parts as if there were no difference between the completeness of my body and the partialness of hers until we fell exhausted into my little bed where, spooned like spent lovers in my little bed, we found ourselves sweetly exploring our clumps and our clefts, the illicit smooth cup of her nub. I loved her, I tell you—and I *did*—but for our sameness, not our difference, the way one completed the other and made us both whole.

Everything happened so fast.

As far as I can remember, one day we were playing in the bath, sculpting bubbles to fill out our flat chests and the missing part of her; the next, subtle shifts between us strained our fond communions. Was that a bud of breast on her soapy bosom? Did she reach now for her sweater in the night because she was cold, or did the cold affect her nub in a way she didn't want me to see? We'd never hidden anything from each other before—why were we suddenly changing clothes in my closet, first her, then me?

A night came that I dreamed I was dancing until all my parts were flying about. Later, I dreamed of my father hunched over and struggling to speak through a smooth white patch where his mouth should have been.

You should never tell your dreams, that much I know.

One day a boy in middle school broke from his noisy herd to shove me up against the wall with a fake choke-hold, pressing his face so close to mine I could feel the pant of his breath, and for days I could think of nothing but the gleam of spit on his teeth, the little brass buckle on his belt, his hot hands. And how could a girl's forbidden lack compare to something like that?

All those years I'd helped her hide it, sewing special garments for her with modest, if not fashionable, coverage and secret pockets she could stuff with Kleenex, but now, why couldn't she buy her clothes where the rest of us shopped, altering them as best she could? When a teacher assigned a team project, wasn't it better to try someone new? And after her mother was gone, it wasn't like it was with the family down the street, for despite the empty places at our tables we all kept for unexpected guests, there was nothing unexpected to her now. When she was little, my new father said, you almost didn't notice, but he sounded like he missed the larger towns and cities to the south where things were more developed, not like here.

And so, it wasn't long before we began to wonder why we'd kept her to begin with. She'd been pleasing enough as a child, but who would want her now? Her clumsiness no longer seemed endearing, and we could see it was not without pain. Sometimes, we noticed, she winced. Sometimes, we did things to cause this.

Once, she tried to tell me something in the street. We were in high school then with our poufy hair and painted lips, but not her. Her lips were as colorless as water, her hair as flat as our chests once were. I tried to pretend I didn't see her, but she reached out to stop me, and what I did—what *could* I do? I looked directly at her nub, not her, and then I walked away.

In this way, the years went by. We had our youthful rites of passage—our first kisses, our proms, our graduations. Two by two, we married. Our children were born whole or not, and we kept them, or not, depending. In truth, I have no memory of those years—my own intact children were small and full of small child demands. They had their milestones and croups, their first days of school, their broken bones and teeth and, later, hearts. And I nursed or celebrated them as the occasions called for, but was never unaware of her, who remained among us if all alone now in her mother's house, and of what keeping her had cost us in the end.

Sometimes, I think about that aloneness—how immense it must have seemed, its persistence. But I still don't know why she did what she did. My father was against her from the start, why should she be for him?

By the time the girl—no longer a girl but a crippled old woman with an acrid scent—strode out to find my father and the others, she had an appearance of purpose that would have put anyone off. The morning she left, she rose before dawn, clattering about in her little house, muttering curses or prayers. We could hear her, everyone could—everyone, at least, who did not cover their ears, for of course, there was nothing sweet about her now.

When she finally emerged, she wore an orange backpack with bright fluorescent stripes and a blue plastic hose for drinking water that snaked up the side of her neck. We could tell from the way she'd packed it that she meant to be gone for a good, long while, yet not one of us moved to say goodbye or stop her. We watched her through our slatted blinds, and we let her go.

On her way out of town, she paused in front of my house, staring staunchly at my bolted door and chewing on a blade of yellow grass. Watching her, I forgot for the first time in years about her missing part and thought, instead, how I had loved her as a child. I remembered the bitterness of my father's denunciations that had done nothing to protect him in the end. I thought about the slim spoon of her body cupped in mine. I thought all this and, thinking it, was on the verge of calling out to her, when suddenly her mouth formed the shapes of words I could not hear. Then she shifted the pack on her back and turned to move on.

Later that morning, we gathered at her house to survey the mess she'd left behind.

And after everything we did for her, one of us harrumphed.

But most of us stood slack-jawed and gaped, for strewn about her little house were scraps of paper everywhere scribbled with notes and bits of maps and careful calculations, and along one whole wall, mechanical drawings of replacement parts. Each of the notes that littered her house began with a name, but despite all the spare parts we had rattling about like useless cogs, not one of ours was among them.

Account C

Among us lived a boy who suffered from a nagging cough.

We first noticed it when he was an infant in his crib plagued by small attacks of hacking, although his mother always said it started in the womb.

Some babies hiccough, she said. This one coughed. It hacked me up inside and never stopped.

If the boy were in the room when his mother said this, he'd crook his arm over his mouth (for he always did cover the right way, with his elbow or a cloth) and cough, but discreetly, perhaps a bit embarrassed. Those of us who knew him were not unsympathetic, but because his coughing fits would come on without warning—in study hall or gym class or field trips to nature—we were forced, in our own way, to avoid him. And since our teachers held him back from any vigorous activity and our parents were reluctant to include him on our playdates, in this we had plenty of assistance, leaving the boy to spend his childhood alone, struggling to master his cough.

But the cough would not be mastered. The cough rose at random from the back of his throat or deep in his chest, a sudden, inexorable force of *something* expelling itself from his body out into our air. No one really knew what that *something* was, yet it filled us with a certain dread for contagion, even then, was already deeply feared. So when the cough came, we did what anyone would do—we masked up (or held our breath) and turned away. We were not unkind, but we were prudent. An ounce of prevention is what we always said.

When all the boy ever wanted was what anyone would want—some little companionship to get him through his days and, in time, perhaps a family of his own. But since desire was the one thing that could really stir his cough up, he did not dare to hope for much and tried, really tried, to strip himself of want, although in this he achieved only modest success. He foreswore his sweet tooth and kept his taste in everything from fashion to lodging homespun and modest in the extreme, but despite its deleterious effects, he proved utterly incapable of lessening his longing for love.

You want someone. I want someone. We are human, after all.

But so was he.

Unmoved, we went about our rituals, our ways of seeking soulmates to take as our cherished companions through all the little joys and tribulations of life. But while we couldn't stop him from trying to join in—filling out the questionnaires that told us who would be compatible with whom and showing up at our mixers in spiffy new clothes—his hands would go all clammy reaching out to say hello, and then, of course, he'd cough. And who could be compatible with that?

Same thing online, for while plenty of us felt a little quickening of the heart when we read the things he wrote, right away, our first phone date: *cough, cough, cough.*

At least on the phone you could just hang up.

Sometimes he even went to the movies, hoping to strike up a conversation with the person in the bubble next to his, but as soon as we saw what bubble he was in, we started shuffling ours about to make a kind of *cordon sanitaire* between him and us. This was supposed to make us feel better, but really, it did not because then we had to look at him surrounded by all those empty bubbles. We were cautious, but not mean, so when the lights went down, we slipped out and got our money back.

The boy was not sick. He did not have germs. Except for the cough, he appeared to be robust, if not athletic. In all other respects, he was generally congenial, kind to animals and pleasant in his interactions with us, no matter how we treated him.

My cough, he apologized in ration queues and waiting rooms where we sometimes found ourselves together, is not contagious. It will never—*cough, cough, cough*—be your cough or do you any harm.

Sadly, in this he would prove to be wrong.

Over time, the boy, now a man, began, like most of us, to mellow. His cough didn't really let up, but he seemed to come to terms with it, to accept it almost like a lover who would never disappoint him or cause him real pain. Despite its persistence, his cough (unlike the ones we all had now, for it was getting tough to breathe) did not burn his throat or cause his chest to ache. He was still alone, of course, but increasingly, we all were. And while the maladies that had begun to afflict us bent us over or sent us to our beds, the boy, now a man, continued to be radiant and thrive. Oh, sure, he could still be awakened in the night by a fit of hacking, but it seemed now to leave him not depleted, but refreshed, as if something—not love, but something like it—had passed through and out of him—to us.

Not that he could have used the word "us," but we could, for who among us had not noticed his empathic glances, the compassion in his eyes as we all began to struggle. He could see how bad things were for us and tried to offer comfort (after all, he'd been there first), but the worse things got for us, the more we held his peace with human suffering against him.

Just look at him, we thought, not without some bitterness. Cough it up, cough it out.

Still, we could not—we just *could not*—act on our suspicions (indeed, our hopes) and ask him to forgive us: What if we proved to be wrong?

Then, in his final days, a strange thing happened. There weren't so many of us left, but we all heard it anyway, the quiet that came on as his cough began to leave him, a subtle thing at first—we'd be standing in a line behind—*far* behind—him, primed to grab our masks for a cough that never came, then, more and more, an eerie silence from his house, a great absence of coughing, until one night we woke up and knew it was gone. As one, we went to check on him who had once been a boy with a nagging cough but was now a very old man, all of us together gathered at his bedside. I was the first one to do it—to poke him—oh so very gently. I poked him on the chest. He didn't move or make a sound—he didn't even cough—but there was such serenity to him that I found myself suddenly engulfed by a memory from grade school.

There's a red rubber ball and the rest of us, coyly ringed in a closed circle, kicking it back and forth to each other. There's a tree, sunbaked asphalt—sticky with heat—and me, as ever, the clumsiest child. Kick, stop, kick; kick, stop, kick. My turn is coming, and now it is here. There is no pleasure in this, but that ball is coming fast, so I close my eyes and swing my leg like always, inauspiciously grazing the top of the ball such that it waggles a few feet, then stops. Flushed with the shame of my clumsiness, I step up to try again, this time surprising us all with a dead center smack that sends the ball off on a course of its own—out beyond our circle, across the playground and the grass, to where the boy is standing in the dim shade of our single tree, the white mask we make him wear clinging damply to the bottom of his face. We know that he knows not to touch what we touch, but the ball is coming straight to him, so he does what anyone would do: He stops it with his foot, and then he kicks it back. He does this with surprising finesse that, surely, we'd have noticed and *admired* if he hadn't started coughing right then. So of course, we run shrieking away.

Now, the whole of our collective lifetimes later, we circled again at the side of his bed, each of us reaching out to poke him. One by one, the feeling rose to overcome us, not so much shame but regret. How few of us were left to see this! I'm not saying I am proud of what I did, but what choice did I have? And so, at last I went to take his cough in as my own, swallow it whole like a red rubber ball of the *something* that rose one last time from his chest when I knelt at his side and put my mouth to his—*lip to lip*—thinking only of how different things would be if I'd allowed myself to do this when we were young instead and full of promise.

Account T

We didn't like looking at them. Looking at them hurt our eyes, whereas looking at us was generally pleasing, although it was hard to say where the differences lay. In all the normative categories—height, weight, number of fingers and toes and holes—us, them, pretty much the same. As such, the qualities that made it us-vs-them were of such a subtle nature it took a while for us to notice them at all.

And of course, they were useful and all, for didn't our lawns need to be mowed, our kitchen floors mopped, our children cared for? Who, if not them, would do this for us?

Don't talk like that, you told me. Talking like that is not nice.

Which, even if I didn't know exactly what you meant, I still went along with it because I'm the agreeable type. Looking back, if you'd just let me talk the way I liked, nothing would have had to change. We could have had our drinks any way we wanted—one day on my lawn, the next on yours. We could have been serene as rain, the way we were supposed to be!

Of course, at first it was just dribs and drabs, the way they came, a few at a time, sometimes a family, as if one more wouldn't matter, which back then it didn't. Then they started pouring in every bit as if they had a right to be here too, and while it didn't happen overnight, that's what it felt like—like everything was different and you couldn't catch your breath and there was nothing you could do about it now because they were already here. Which is to say not quite *among* us—that wouldn't do—but far too close. It was hard to believe this could happen here, but we were getting short on space and look at them—they just kept coming. Surely, someone should have stopped it at first notice of their difference—their shapes and tones and appetites—flat, where we were round; blunt, where we were sharp.

Distinctly, too, there was an odor wafting from them which, to be fair, was not exactly *malodorous*, but neither did it smell a bit like us. Our odor was savory and biscuit-y, and when push comes to shove, who doesn't like biscuits?

The list was long, with new things added every day.

The things they ate. The way they talked. The clothes their children wore.

We didn't like thinking like this. Thinking like this gave us an overall low, grim feeling—we used to be so open-minded and all.

When we were little—for naturally, we were once little—we thought about our playthings and our schoolbooks. We thought about what we would be when we grew up.

And then, like that, we did.

It was a long time since either of us had given any thought to childish things.

Now, we found ourselves trying to remember.

My plaything was a tattered goat; my schoolbook had numbers in it.

Neither had we thought much about numbers, except for keeping track of us-vs-them, from which we knew that one day not so far from now there would be more of them than us!

It all depended on how you looked at things, you said.

Or them, I said, on how you looked at *them*.

But because I knew exactly what you meant, even if I acted like I didn't, I looked around at how things were, and here's what I wanted: I wanted to sleep.

I dreamed of a house that took five hours to walk from one end to the other in down a long corridor that went on for miles, the ceiling above, as high as the sky. When I saw that, I sighed a sigh of such relief, as here, I thought, there will be room for everyone. We can live in comfort and visit whenever the mood strikes. We will not be alone. But neither will we be crammed tight together. We will have our space.

In this way, I become the architect of the house I dream.

On one end of the corridor, a lovely suite of spacious rooms and great cathedral windows that flood the rooms with yellow light and overlook a rocky bluff and wild sea. On the other, a vast basilica—or vault—of chiseled stone without any windows at all. It is bare, with nothing in it. And it is cold and dank. But it is big!

When you walk into the first room, you know you are at home, with easy chairs and ottomans to put your feet up and gaze out on the open sea and a great white bed for sleep.

But when you walk into the second, an immense expanse of nothing.

You in your room and me in mine.

But which is which, you want to know: Which room do I get, and which do you?

Maybe you said this and maybe you didn't, but we both knew you were thinking it. And the thinking caused a little stab of envy and resentment to grow inside our hearts. Why did *I* always get the nicest things? Why did *I* always get to choose first?

I thought about the bare vault on the other end of the long, dark corridor. I thought about its bareness, and I thought about its vastness. Fair is fair, and right is right, but that's not what I said.

Here's what I said: But we could fix it up, wait and see. We could get some La-Z-Boys and knock a window out to fill your great basilica with light, like mine. We could get a bike!

Notice, I said *basilica*, not *vault*.

Another word for *vault* is *dungeon*, which neither of us said.

But once we punched the hole out for the window, where would we get the glass, you sniffed, and what would be my view?

Not a wild seashore but a set of ragged steps to a crowded tourist cove. Just look at them streaming past the window in their gaudy tourist hats! Below, they stretch their oily bodies on the sand so close together that if one turns over, the rest flip too, greasy as tinned fish and seared from the sun, playing tacky tourist music, eating tacky tourist food.

Between us both, the little stab of envy and resentment was beginning to fester. You were the one who wanted to talk nice—what need would you have for windowpanes? Let the wind blow in! Things could be worse.

In the dream, I declared that I didn't mind a wit; it could still go either way. Say the word, I said: *You* choose. But we both knew that I did mind—the lovely suite with rocky bluffs and wild surf belonged to me and me alone; for you, the vault and hoi-polloi. Up any corridor as long and as wide as the corridor in my dream, no odors could waft their slimy way. You in your room and me in mine, that was the way it all made sense.

You can hear them! You can smell them! How will I ever sleep? you whined.

But of course, there'd be no sleep for us. Sleep was a thing of the distant past. Sleep was for the world the way it was when we were young, you in your bed and me in mine.

Your plaything was a rubber ball; your schoolbook was a tome of poems.

Maybe their smell was somehow musty. Musty isn't so bad, I guess, per se.

But did I mention they were increasing in number? Did I say they were still pouring in? And some of them were small. Commensurately, their smell was only going to get worse. You couldn't escape the truth of that.

Small, we knew, does not stay small.

And so, in the absence of sleep, no dreams. No robots, no sex toys, no albatrosses. A time is coming, sooner and sooner, when even this small remaining order will no longer hold. You will want my tattered goat, and I will want your ball. When that time comes, I want you to remember this: We didn't need the lovely suite that overlooked the rocky shore; we didn't need the windows with either of their views. What we needed, you and me, was *us*.

We could have lived outside in tents.

We could have been content.

If not, you must remember this, for what to do to them.

Account F3

There wasn't anything outwardly wrong with the child who appeared in our great hall that day.

Well, except that we couldn't quite tell if it was a boy or a girl. This was before the he—or the she—was removed from their jacket, like all of us once were removed from ours. But not before we checked to be sure—ten little tips of fingers poking out from the ends of the sleeves and, from the trousers, ten little toes. Everything right as rain in that regard, so of course it was exciting, someone new like that. What did the rest of it matter? Removed of our names along with our jackets, it wasn't so easy to tell with us either, although I certainly knew my which from my what. I was clear as could be about that.

They called it a great hall, but really, it was just a big room.

At the end of the room, a pane in the wall that we called a window, too high to see anything out of.

In the room, us.

Removed of our jackets, we got smocks instead; removed of our names, we got numbers.

Evens slept on the right, odds on the left. I was an even, so being in the right came naturally to me. Beside your bed, a little chest—evens on the right, odds on the left. Here's what we had to keep in our chests: one little gray smock to wear in the day and one little gray smock for the night, something to clean our teeth and something to dry our face after we washed with our one bar of soap, a jar to keep our numbers in, and the other thing they gave us to cover the parts of our bodies it was the rule to keep covered. Some of us had a few other things which, for some reason, we had not been removed of—buttons off the jacket of a person once beloved, cards with pictures on them you could use to play a game, tiny teeth. No one knew whose teeth they were, but they were pretty—and sharp. What I had was a little brush with the softest whitest bristles in the world even though they didn't let us have hair. Hair was all tangles and lice, they said, as they removed us of ours.

What's lice? we said.

Ha, they said. You're welcome.

That was the first thing we really did notice—how the new child had something like what might be called hair, a kind of peachy fuzz that glistened on the top of his or her head all the way down to the nape of the neck. But how could this be? Hair wasn't allowed.

It's not as if they didn't try. They took the child the same as us into the room where they did what they did to remove us of whatnots, and then they returned him or her, smooth at the top as a spoon or an egg, which gave us all a subtle sense of vindication.

Ha, we thought, not without ambivalence. No one gets hair.

Shortly after, a collective gasp: The fuzz was back!

You wouldn't think it could happen so fast.

Seeing the fuzz, I didn't quite know how to feel, but one thing I did know, a brush was for hair, and I had a brush. Whatever I remembered of hair back then, maybe someone washed it, or brushed it with soft bristles, or ran their hands through it in a kind or loving way. But what did I know? Maybe my brush was for a doll. We didn't know why they let some things slip in. They just did. One boy had a piece of licorice as old as kingdom come, and what wouldn't some of the rest of us do to get our hands on that! So of course, this made me worry: What wouldn't this new child do to get his or her hands on my brush?

The next thing that happened is hard to explain. As soon as the new crown of fuzz appeared, they took the child to perform the removal over again. We'd all had it done—oh, yes we had!—which, there being nothing gentle about it, most of us hoped, never again. But with the new boy or girl, the fuzz on the top of his or her head that wasn't quite hair but not not-hair either kept coming back. No one knew why. It was almost as if the new boy or girl was doing it on purpose, which we couldn't help but wonder, if the child could do that, what other remainders or whatnots might he or she have lying in store for us? Sadly, we thought of our whatnots. Just like with hair, no one gets those.

All this went on for a while, back and forth, hair/no-hair, until one day, without any warning, the child was discharged from the temporary holding place, where all of us stayed throughout our transitions to learn the rules and be fitted for smocks and removed of impermissible things, and delivered to us same as always—teeth, toes, little smock—but—and it's hard to say this even now—with a letter, not a number.

And again, the collective gasp: What were we to do with that?

But the tag on the front of the smock was clear, so after the gasp, a quiet shuffling of feet. The letter on the tag was M which, coming as it did at the center of the alphabet, neither odd nor even and as much mountain as valley, left us flummoxed. There was M, standing all alone in the doorway with his or her bed and little chest. We didn't even think to wonder what was in it yet. All we were wondering was where we should put it.

Being an even, I had my own opinion and was about to share it when all at once—and sure, we should have seen this coming too—M started shoving his or her bed all the way down the center of the room, between the odds and evens, to the one and only spot beneath what we called a window. By now, one thing was certain: No one wanted M on their side of the room, but no one wanted M to have the window either. And, of course, there was the matter of the chest.

So here's what happened next: M marched back to the doorway for his or her chest and shoved it—unaided by any of us—all the way down to the foot of the bed. And then M did another thing we'll never forget: M jumped on the bed, kicked his or her feet up toward the ceiling, and laughed—or chortled—*ha ha, tee hee, heh heh*—like it was the happiest day of M's life.

But chortle or laugh, we saw now how things were going to be: Beds were for nighttime, for sleeping your flat dreamless sleep and keeping your chest beside and in the chest, your things. You weren't supposed to jump on them, not ever, but especially not now in the middle of the day, rumpling its covers, undoing its neatness. Day was for tidiness, for doing your chores or lessons in, for observing somber interludes of quiet contemplation. *Quiet*, not chortling or laughing. Rules were rules, same as hair.

These concerns were so much on most of our minds that we almost missed the pure pleasure in what M was doing, if we had words for it, which we did not.

And that was that.

Not that we leapt on our beds and messed them up too—that's not the kind of thing that ever could have happened. But whatever we might have done to move M away from the window was moot now. That's where M's bed was, and that's where M's bed was going to stay.

Now that M was among us, we noticed that the fuzz had a kind of earthy smell to it like soap, maybe, but not our soap, some other kind of soap, some soap for hair that we didn't dare to think came from *elsewhere*. This got me thinking, and while I don't know what got the others thinking, something did—the rumpled bed, the gleam of fuzz, the memory of windows you could see through, even the color of M's smock, not quite the same color as ours, close enough but maybe from a different herd of sheep.

The thing about M being right in the middle of the room between the odds and the evens, with the gleam of fuzz and smell of something not from here and the rumpling of bedcovers in the middle of the day, well, of course we were curious. Moreover, although we didn't want to say so, we felt our curiosity somewhere in our bodies that we never felt before. Not right away, but over time, it's hard to know quite how to put this, that curiosity began to exert a kind of pull on us. It was subtle at first but hard to ignore, an equal pull on all of us, both right and left.

There M was in the middle of the room, and there we were, in our beds on either side.

And of course, the feeling that we had grew more insistent as time passed. We all felt this, both evens and odds. No one wanted to talk about it, but since we were all feeling it—feeling *curious*, the way we were—it shouldn't have been that hard to predict that the longer we felt it, the stronger it got—the tug or pull of it—until, like an itch, we just had to scratch it. For some of us, the feeling got strong all at once, and they were the first. But the rest of us weren't far behind. Pretty soon, we all had to do it. And pretty soon, all of us were.

During the day, we went on like always—lessons, chores, somber contemplation. But then at night it started up, the quiet pattering of feet, from either left or right, all the way down to the end of the room where the gold fuzz gleamed in what we called the moonlight. And then a little later, the pattering back.

Of course, we knew how very wrong this was. If daytimes were not for jumping on beds, nighttimes were not for traipsing about by the light of whatever it was that shone through what we called a window to do something in M's bed other than sleep. Everyone knew this—*I* knew this.

But we couldn't stop ourselves. The fuzz was there, and so were we.

Being an even, I took my time. No matter how curious I might be or how much I might want to join in with the pattering of feet, you weren't supposed to do it, so I didn't. I held out as long as I could.

One by one, the others got up in the dead of the night and pattered all the way down to where M was stretched in his or her bed, fuzz agleam in the light.

Sometime later, they made their way back.

In the end, I was one of the last, or maybe the last one of all. I had the same feelings as everyone else, but I knew the rules.

Still, if you listen long enough to the furtive pattering of feet—*back and forth, back and forth*—and then one night, it stops—when you're one of the last ones or maybe the last one of all—you can't really stop yourself.

No one could, and neither could I.

So that's when I got myself up. I shook the sheet off and swung my legs out of the bed and put my bare feet on the icy floor and walked all the way down to where M lay awake on the bed in the middle of the room removed of his or her smock and looking exactly—and not at all—as I had imagined and oh so very pale in the light of what we called the moon, utterly bare and wholly revealed to me. But it wasn't his boy-ness or her girl-ness— or not-boyness nor not-girlness either—that made me feel the horrible force of the awe that came over me then. We were plenty used to that by now. It was, instead, his or her whiteness—snow white, chalk white, bleached white, bone white—topped off with that little shimmer of gold.

I don't know how to tell you what it felt like. Most of the others already knew, so by the time I was finding out, we were almost to the end anyway. All I know is that touching that fuzz was unlike touching anything I had ever felt before and that, even as I touched it, I knew it was the last time in my life I would ever feel anything like it. I could tell how depleted M was from all the touching. So sure, maybe if I'd waited. I could have waited. Everyone else had had their turn. What would it have hurt me to wait a little more?

I was never among those who said "chortle," but as I approached this all-white and gleaming thing with its crown of gold fuzz in the not at all neat anymore bed at the far end of the room where what we called a window shed all we knew of light, I remembered the sound of her or his laugh that first time she or he leapt on their bed, mussing it up in the middle of the day, but not mussed like this—all stained and smelly—mussed different. And now, at last, I thought to wonder for what would be the first but not the last time what accounted for the joy of him or her that day: Why was M so happy to be among us? Happy, like pleasure, was not a word we knew to think yet, or not me, but I would soon enough because I was almost to the bed now, I was almost already touching M's fuzz.

And then, like that, it was done.

———

After they found out and M was removed from us, they let us have hair, but that's all they let us have. That's how we learned about tangles and lice. That's how we learned you can only know something from what it is not.

Looking back, I think the hardest thing to lose was not the bed and not the chest, and not even my dear soft-white-bristled brush, but the little gray smocks they made us wear, the one for day, the one for night, along with the other thing for covering parts of our bodies we didn't yet know to keep covered.

That was the first thing we learned, but not the last, after they sent us away removed of everything, all the way down to our numbers.

Account M

One time I ran into that girl who used to live across the street. I looked up and there she was, looking at me.

I remember the time you stole the milk can from our front porch, she said.

I said, it wasn't a can, it was a *jar*. And I didn't steal it, I borrowed it. That's different.

She paused, then added, a bit slyly, at least you admit that you took it.

That's when I knew that she knew. I knew it from the way she said it, lacking curiosity or judgment. And she was right. I took it. I took it from the porch back in the time when people still had things other people could take and porches for things to be on. I wouldn't do anything different. You can't change what's happened. But she didn't really want to talk about it. Accuse, condemn, denounce. That's what she wanted. She was big now, with a flat face where you could see traces of what had gone on and inside her mouth, a snag of broken teeth, sheared almost in half.

Yet she was the one accusing me of taking a thing I had meant to return.

I took it for the bugs. It was there, on the porch, so I took it.

The foil thing to put over the hole at the top was missing, but the neck was narrow so you could stuff it with almost any old rag or wad of paper or leaves or leftover sock. My plan was to use leaves since someone might notice if I took a rag or wad of paper and the mate to the sock could show up, but then I thought what if the bugs ate the leaves? Who knew what the bugs were going to eat, once they were here? All we knew was that they were coming. They were going to be coming out of the ground. They had been coming for years, and now was their time. I can't say we were ready. Who can be ready for something like bugs? On the inside of our houses, we lay on our little beds or whined about our chores, but on the outside, we sat on our porches and watched the ground for signs of bugs. We knew from pictures they'd have great, bulbous eyes, transparent wings, and gold-stippled bodies, but would they be moist or dry or soft or crunchy? Would they have a smell?

We didn't know yet to worry about the sound of them and how it would fill the air around us and never stop, a terrible buzzing that started on the outside of our ears but then worked its way into our bodies and brains until we weren't the same anymore. We were different. And we always would be.

But that was still going to be after the bugs had come, which they hadn't yet. Now, we were waiting. It was summer. We were hot and riddled with the doldrums, and the jar, like I said, was there.

It wasn't a dare, per se, more like a pact I had with some others, something we thought up one night with nothing to do but think things up: If I filled a jar with the bugs, the others would eat them. And I could watch. That's what they said.

But I didn't have a jar. Our parents had jars for keeping things in—buttons and string and farfalline. But all our jars already contained things, and where would I put the things if I took them out to make room for bugs? Where would I *hide* them? What if they were missed?

Other than that, we didn't have empty jars lying around. Everything you had, you used, even then.

The others were boys.

Despite the drifting idleness of summer, there was a certain urgency to my jar quest because another thing we knew was that, as sure as the bugs were coming, they wouldn't last long. They had their cycle, and we had ours. We, being singular creatures of our own, were born on the face of the earth to live out our misery or lack of it for an indeterminate number of years, unique to each of us; whereas the bugs all lived and died together at once. This was the nature of hives. Humans weren't hives yet but bugs were, which meant that if you were a bug, you would never be alone, but you were also just part of the hive, with your stages and metamorphoses, being born, for example, deep inside the earth, where you lived your secret life for the eternity of seventeen Earth years in complete darkness until it was time for you to come out—all of you together, burrowing up to the light and air—to *us!*—so as to sing songs of love to each other, so as to mate, so as to die.

The last time the bugs came, I was not even born yet. All my life, I'd been waiting for them.

Everyone knew they were coming, so we waited.

I saw the milk jar on the porch, so I took it.

I don't know why I wanted this—for them to eat the bugs, for me to watch.

They were boys, and I was not. They ran around and punched each other and rolled on the ground, letting out shrieks in the night and farting for fun. Inside their hard muscular bodies, powerful sinews rippled. Whereas my body was soft and small, my manner peaceable and pliant. I had my smell, vanilla; they had theirs, a little skunky. And now they said that if I gave them bugs—a whole jarful—they would eat them, and I could watch.

At first, I wasn't sure. They sniggered when they said this, as if there were something to snigger about. When the bugs came, who knew what it was going to be like? But the more I thought about it—and I thought about it a lot—the more I thought it was something I did want. It gave me this feeling, just thinking about it, somewhere deep inside my body, a feeling like that. Don't ask me why.

The girl across the street ate a worm once. She didn't know I was watching from the little upstairs bedroom where I slept at night and got dressed in the morning, tied my shoes, thought my thoughts. My parents had a bedroom downstairs to be closer to the door just in case. Even though we were supposed to keep the curtains drawn, I could still peek out the crack, so I watched her. What else was there to do? She was digging around in the dirt with her finger, not a shovel or a spoon, and the look on her face, as if she were digging for something. After a while, she pulled it out, a long, thin, stringy thing that wriggled—or *spasmed*—as she dangled it close to the front of her face.

Then she puckered up her lips and sucked the stringy thing through them in a slow, intentional way. And when she was done, she went inside her house.

Maybe it wasn't a worm, but it was a long, thin, stringy thing that came out of the ground and wriggled. I don't know why she did this. No one was watching except for me behind the curtains inside my house. Other than that, we were pretty much alike, her in her house and me in mine. We didn't have much, but it was enough. We had our milk, our farfalline. We had houses with porches to go on and off, rooms to sleep in with curtains to peek through. On the outside, boys shoved each other and ran around sniggering. We knew the difference between borrowing and stealing. We knew bugs were coming.

Maybe you wonder how we knew these things—about the bugs and borrowing and stealing. But if I tell you school or parents, you'll just want to know what's that. The thing you need to know about parents—the *only* thing you need to know—is they are big, and you are small. That's all there is and all there is ever going to be, as if bigness alone can provide for or protect you. Also, who built the porch, if not the parents? Who gets the milk?

Whereas small can hide under your bed and not make a peep.

I don't really know how we knew the bugs were coming. Books, parents, something told us. We *knew*, is all. Maybe we *remembered* it inside our bodies. Everybody's bodies were ripe with this feeling of waiting that made some people want to eat bugs and others watch and others, I don't know what. At night, in my bed, I could hear the low murmur of them deep inside the earth, but burrowing up, up, toward the light and air—toward *me*.

Maybe the boys knew something I didn't. Or maybe they were hungry. I don't know, and I don't care. All I know is what they made me do.

The bugs came. There was no surprise in this. One morning, we peeked outside our windows and the ground was rippling—*shuddering*—with something about to break through.

Oh, oh, we cried, come see!

We called this to our big parents who came to the windows inside our houses and said, it's only bugs; they won't hurt you. Come, drink your milk and close the curtains.

But of course, we knew it was bugs! That's what we'd been waiting for this whole time!

The milk was warm and left a fat and furry feeling on our tongues and lips as, just outside our houses, the earth itself was stirring until, finally all at once, it burst open with them, the bugs freed upon us at last. They had red bulbous eyes, like we knew they would, but the stippling of their bodies was more chartreuse than golden; their wings, a shimmery kind of transparency that was no real color at all. But the big surprise was how noisy they were, the terrible buzzing they made not from their voice box but from rubbing the parts of their bodies together without ever stopping, and the sound was so loud it pumped my head full and I couldn't think about anything else—not my big mother and father, not my little bed, not the girl and her worm, not even the milk jar under my bed where I put it when I took it from the porch across the street. It smelled sour, like the milk it held inside it would make your stomach hurt even more than it already did.

The buzzing was their mating song. We know that now.

By the time I remembered the boys and my jar, everything outside was covered with bugs—the mailbox, covered; the fence, covered; the old sycamore tree and the place where cars used to park, all covered. By covered I mean black because despite being bright and colorful when they were open and flying about, when the bugs stopped to rest—and *mate*—they folded up into a dark and pulsing blackness like a premature and inauspicious dusk. This gave me second thoughts, but a pact was a pact. At least there were so many it wasn't going to be hard to fill my jar. If I had a bucket or a bowl or a big soup ladle, I could scoop them up easy-peasy and be done. But who had things like that? I would have to use my hands. And I would have to go outside to the inside of their pulsing, which was everywhere and nowhere at once. I am not sure how to put this, but it filled me with what I only know to call a hollowness. And *oh, oh*, who can bear to be hollow and full at once?

These are the things I was thinking as I crawled under my bed to fish out the jar and go catch bugs.

What I wasn't thinking—what I didn't expect—was not the flat wall of noise that hit me as soon as I opened the door, the whole world undulating with a kind of heartbeat, but the crunching that was going to happen under my feet when I stepped off the porch and out into them. Nor did I think ahead about how, even though we had milk to drink and curtains to peek through, I was still in between shoes. No point to new shoes when the next bigger size is coming up around the corner, it being summer and all, your feet will toughen up by and by. Which, really, they did not, and so I'd feel it all, every bit of it—the brittle shell of exoskeleton splintering beneath my feet, the goo from their insides squishing up between my toes the exact same temperature of the day itself. Or maybe you wouldn't think that the bugs would crunch beneath feet as small and as soft as mine, or why didn't I shove them out of my path with my foot and not step on them at all? But there were so many, and if I tried to push them aside, they swarmed up around me, flapping their wings at my legs and face and tangling up in my hair, so no clearing of the path—*no*. Just the slimy, sticky progress of my *crunch, crunch, crunch*, all the way to the mailbox where I thought it would be easy to pluck the bugs off the top and plop them into my jar.

But did you know about the mouthparts—the long, thin, stringy things that come out from the inside of their mouths to pierce plants and suck up their sap and do the same to you when you pick the bugs up to shove into your jar because who has a ladle or a bowl? You have to take them by their wings and pinch between your fingers so they don't fly away, but the long thin stringy things loop back anyway and stab into you, along with the others that crawl up your legs and into your shorts and down your neck and under your top until, like the mailbox or the fence or the whole rest of the world, you are black with bugs too, a great pulsing husk of bug yourself, all with their mouthparts seeking out the most tender parts of you. It doesn't hurt, per se, but you can feel it, the long thin stringy thing making a tiny prick in your skin and then probing around inside you to suck the secret juice as if you were a plant. And when it comes out, a little red spot, like a kiss, that will start to itch soon. And if your jar is big with a small opening, it will take a long time to fill—so long, that soon, your hand, then your arm, then the whole rest of your body is speckled with tiny red spots from the long thin stringy things coming out of their mouths to pierce your skin and suck from the inside of you something not sap.

I don't know why it meant so much to me to watch those boys eat bugs. I could watch them eat all kinds of things we weren't supposed to eat any old time I wanted. I could watch them eat dirt and toothpaste and the slimy insides of fish you could sometimes find down by the water. They were boys who ran around and got so hungry they'd eat anything at all because unless you're very small, you can't live on milk alone. If all you eat is milk, after a while, you probably die.

I don't know where the milk came from. I can't even say now it was really milk. Maybe we just called it milk. It came in those jars and made your mouth fat and furry, which was at least a distraction from your tummy.

By the time my jar was full of bugs, I was spotted all over and didn't know, either, if anything was left on the inside of me from everything the long, thin, stringy mouthparts were sucking out, but maybe they were putting something back too. Thinking this gave me a light-headed feeling that wasn't yet pain—that, the pain would come later. And the smell of crunched bugs was an acrid something in my nose that *did* hurt. If those boys were going to eat them, they better be quick because even though we knew that living things—*all* living things—were protein, those bugs weren't going to live forever inside my jar and then think how bad they were going to smell.

I filled my jar. Then I took it back to the inside of my house. And now I know that is the one thing I shouldn't have done. Not taking the jar in the first place, not making the pact with the boys. Not even filling the jar up with bugs while the inside of me was being sucked out and filled up from the mouthparts with something not me.

So, when that girl said what she said, how I stole the jar, when I understood she knew what I had done—knew it, but without curiosity or judgment, just a flatness that proved everything that happened was my fault, I meant what I said—I was going to return it. It was for the boys to do what they said, and then I was going to bring it back.

You think because your mother and your father—your *parents*—are big, they are completely on your side and will always be there to protect you. Everyone thinks this as long as they can.

But how could I have known what was going to happen when I was still in-between shoes? And why didn't anyone warn me about the outside and the inside? Back then, we could still cross, willy-nilly, over the thresholds of our doors or in and out under our beds because we were the rulers of everything; we built the world we lived in and used up until the bugs came. But once you start mixing up the order of things—the big and small, the inside and the outside, the above and beneath—watch out.

And maybe you think all *lah-de-dah*, it's only bugs. What can happen if you bring the outside bugs to the inside of your home after they've come up from under the ground, especially if you keep them in a milk jar with a wad of leaves or paper so they can't come out again and shake almost all the rest of them off from wherever they crawled on your clothes or body to use their mouthparts on you?

But bugs go outside. I know that now. Bugs go out, and we go in.

Or maybe you think something will happen inside the jar that will make them die first, like you and me living off only milk, even before the boys get to eat them, dead or alive. But dying was what they were doing on the outside—dying was the whole freaking point of it all.

Account A

We weren't sure there was anything left to discuss, so the matter was closed for now: Look outside your window— the animals were back.

How long was it, anyway, since we'd got rid of them?

Such a nuisance they had been, what with their growly barks and gristly furballs, their snarly omnivorous ways: *I'm going to eat you, I'm going to eat you.* Unless, of course, we ate them first.

It wasn't easy routing them the last time. It took forethought and resolve. But fair was fair.

Every morning we awoke to find them rooting in our lawns, as if they were digging for something like water. The mess they made, you can't believe. We had water, sure, but that was for our pansies and petunias, which they also took to eating by and by.

Now, we surveyed the land outside. If there were any lawns left, they'd be in a ruin by now. But even without any lawns, we still tried to keep things as neat as we could.

Naturally, the hardest part of all was how to explain it to the children. Such adorable creatures the children were, their pretty heads covered with fuzz, all cuddly and romping about. These children—*our* children—were the noisiest things around, but what did they have to make noise about? They had all their dear, little teeth by then, but weren't on the verge of losing them yet; their dreams were as gentle as what were once sheep.

Well, sheep were never gentle, but we thought of them like that. Soft wooly lambs with wet black eyes.

Never mind sheep. These nasty comeback animals were not like sheep at all. Was it vengeance? Who could say? All we knew was they were gone and now were back, stinking up our outside and flaunting their proclivities.

Oh, oh, the children cried: I hear something, I smell something, I *see* something.

And what were we supposed to say?

Once, a long time ago, the world was full of creatures with legs and tails that walked and ran and ate and drank and slept and dreamed, just like you. Except where it was covered with water, seas full of beings that breached and swam.

You couldn't tell them that. What happened to those animals? they'd say. When they grew up, they'd think they had a right to know. Their little teeth were firm and straight right now, but one day, they'd fall out, and after that, the ones that come back are sharp and strong. They'd be just like the animals then.

Or else, they'd want to know what a tail was.

What's fur, they'd say, although, in fact, you never mentioned fur.

Fur was a thing of the distant past, you probably wouldn't want to say, like what's on dogs. Because *ooh-la-la*, what's distant past, what's dog?

I had a boy myself once, and my boy had a dog. That boy loved that dog for all the world, and the dog loved the boy. The two of them together were the same as children now, all cuddly and romping about—dog for a pillow, dog for a horse, dog for a hug. The boy had a name for the dog, and the dog had a lick for the boy. We didn't have much, my boy and me, but we had each other, and we had that dog. Shouldn't that have been enough?

I don't know what my boy did to make that dog turn on him. It must have been something. And it served the boy right. But when you saw him all shredded up like that, it still broke your heart, even a tough heart like mine.

So of course, when I saw what was going on outside, I did what we all did and drew the blinds.

As long as you didn't look, you didn't have to see.

Account G2

Perfectly fine the way she is, the doctor declared as he finished his first, most thorough exam, but we knew what we knew. She was our very own, and yet we knew it in our hearts: She was not right.

And what were people going to say about us now?

They were going to say suck it up. She passed the doctor, so go with the flow.

They were going to say it was in our heads, not hers.

But we were there, we tell you. We saw it all. On the outside, everything normal enough, but on the inside, she was weak about the eyes and whistled when she dreamed. Not a whistle of a tune or melody but a hollow flute of air going in and out her breathing pipe every bit as though the dream were playing her.

Also, she was naughty, and she didn't mind. When we told her brush your teeth, she stomped her little feet and her eyes went cold as ice and sharp as something you could use to pick them out with. And we knew, we could just tell there was no command or force on earth that would make her brush her teeth. Same thing when it came to do your homework. She'd run outside instead and start firing lemons up over the fence and into the yard of our neighbors, who we didn't have a single thing against, except the dog. The lemons fell from our tree and were rotten and split open from lying on the ground, but she lobbed them like a piston. She was just a little girl, but she could make them fly.

So you'd take me by the hand and stand me by the window to make me look at her, our very own, not brushing her teeth or doing her homework despite what we told her to do. And then you'd squeeze my hand the way you do as if to say: This is what you wanted, *do* something. And the dog on the other side of our fence going wild from the lemons coming at him out of nowhere: *Bark, bark, bark. Bark, bark, bark.*

I wouldn't say that dog was normal either. It wasn't just lemons that set it off, but any old little thing—the postman, delivery drones, my own washer-dryer ringing out a little ditty to let me know they were done. Our fence was made of cinderblocks, so we never saw that dog, if it was big or small, or what kind of teeth it had. But we could hear it. Even if it wasn't barking, it was running back and forth in a wild frenzy. You could stand there on our side of the fence and hear the pounding of its feet along the hard-packed ground on the other side, the pant of its terrible breath, the slurp of its drool. Mainly, though, it barked—*bark, bark, bark*—keeping the whole neighborhood on edge.

Bark, bark, bark. Bark, bark, bark.

It got so bad I called it in, but they said it had a license for protection. Protection was a right. You could take your pick: gun or razor wire, motion sensor, booby trap, dog. If the dog was for protection, their hands, they said, were tied.

Oh yeah, I thought, not without a good deal of bitterness, well, but what about us?

I was thinking of our girl. On the outside, beware of dog, but on the inside, what was there to protect us from our very own?

You were thinking of her too, so you took my hand and squeezed it the way you do. When it was just the two of us, we did okay. You brought me little treats from the market and every day a flower from the empty house across the street. But oh no, that wasn't enough—I wanted more. Now, even the memory of all that want inside me was too much to bear, so we agreed to say nothing more on the subject ever again. Our lips were sealed: Now we were three.

You think you can control these things. You think you are the master of your fate.

You think I don't know what you mean when you squeeze my hand like that.

You think I wanted this, but this isn't what I wanted, something else: a girl who, when you put a ribbon in her hair, didn't snatch it out and wrap it tight around your neck; a girl who, when the teacher called, it was something good, an award or kindness she had done; a girl who, when the dog barked, ran away from it, not toward it—a normal girl like me.

She had the prettiest toes, though. As pretty as pretty could be.

It was hard to explain it to the doctor, how they curled when the whistling dreams played through her. We took turns standing watch above her bed. The breath that came in on the edge of the whistle was lemony and warm. She was our very own. But the breath that came out on the other side left a cold clutch of dread in our hearts. From her little curling toes and perked-up ears and whistling breath, this is how we knew things were not right, but how could we prove that to the doctor, who tried to tell us all we needed was more sleep?

Her ears were little, too—dear, pink, cunning shells on the two sides of her head that quivered when she whistled like an animal that senses something threatening or tasty. Everything about her was little, although we knew it would not stay that way for long. People never think, when they apply for children, how small and sweet is just a passing phase. One day, she'd be big, like us. We'd be sitting in our places for our dinner—you, me, her—with her coal-black eyeballs staring back at us from across the table and her giant stubs of toes digging scratch marks in our floor. She'd still curl them, though, like knuckles, which we'd feel—oh wouldn't we—when she kicked our shins to get her something that she wanted. And the dreambreath coming out of her will not be warm, but hot.

We knew this. We could see the future coming. The future coming made us feel powerless and small.

A family is four, we used to say: a mother, a father, a sister, a brother.

But what did we know back then?

One is enough, you say now.

She was our very own, so naturally we loved her, despite the curling of her toes and whistling of her breath, the subtle clench of jaw, the perk of ears. She didn't make much noise, but when you saw her tense her body, it conjured up the frenzy of that dog—ominous and very, very scary.

Bark, bark, bark, part and parcel of her dream.

In the morning, she'd wake up and smile almost sweetly. I want milk, she said. Then she demanded: I want *my* milk.

There were other signs as well: When she finished with her bath and ran off naked through the house, the prints her wet feet left had something smudged about them, but despite the smudginess, you could see an extra toe.

So we tried another doctor, down the road a bit.

We said, the dreams this child has, you can't imagine. Terrible things are happening inside her, and if you don't fix her, soon they'll be happening on the outside too.

The doctor peered into her little ears; he checked her eyes; he listened to her breathy breath.

There's a bit of a wheeze, he said finally. Otherwise, perfectly fine.

And then he offered drugs—for us instead of her. And that's when we knew he'd been hoodwinked by her toes.

Well, you said, as if in time you would forgive me, I guess that's that.

And even though I knew you never would, I still said, it's a pity. She's so pretty and all.

When we got home, we told her go to her room, but she went outside, instead, to lob lemons over the fence with gleeful satisfaction.

Here's the kind of satisfaction that I mean: *Bark, bark, bark. Bark, bark, bark.*

The dreams that came out of her mouth on the crest of her whistling breath had nothing to do with the way things were now but how they were going to be. She was our very own, but we could not—we just could *not*—believe the dreams she dreamed. They said she was fine and for us to suck it up. They said it was a phase, she would outgrow it. But it was other people's children who were fine. Other people's children brushed their teeth and did their homework—they *minded*. And when they ran on the floor with wet feet, they left clear little prints with no more than five toes. We knew that much. Other people's children did not have phantom toes left over from their dreams. And soon it would be more than just toes.

We want it to be known that we did everything we could. We were vigilant and thorough. We tried home remedies and discipline, a regular routine, counseling, prayer. We watched over as she slept. And while it could be said we loved her—she was our very own—when the vapors started trailing on the whistling of her dreambreath and the barking never stopped the whole night through, we knew—we just *knew*—what we had to do.

No don't, I said, before you start, as you reached for my hand to squeeze it the way you do. But of course, I agreed you were right: She'd thrown all those lemons, now she'd have to clean them up.

When what I really meant was remember how things were before. It was a little moment, a single shared breath between as we both thought back to what it was like when all in the world I'd wanted was her, and all you had wanted was me.

Account 1

You know what hurt? I'll tell you what hurt. Everything hurt. Starting with our teeth. You could see it in the tightness at the corners of our jaws, the little lines that spread out from our eyes, the clench.

I will relax my teeth, the dentist said to say: I will relax my teeth, like a mantra or a promise, but what did the dentist know?

First, our teeth, then other stuff, too. Our toes, our skin. Do you remember how it seared from the barest brush of the lightest fabrics? You wanted to go naked, and so did I, but we were far too old for that.

Don't touch, you cried. Don't touch.

Don't even breathe on me, I pleaded.

Each morning we woke up to every bit as much space between us as we could get—a whole ocean of bed—you crammed at the far edge of your side of it, me crammed at the far edge of mine, as if space could cure us. But even then, we knew it would never be enough. We needed more.

Instead, we got less.

One day, an inspector came to our door. He had some papers and a kind of tag. I was in the next room, so I heard it all. He wanted to know about the children.

I'm not sure what you mean, you demurred.

Which, really, might not have been the smartest thing. You could have lied. Everyone else did—lying was all the rage back then. But we weren't like everyone else, so you didn't, and I didn't have the sense to run out and lie for you either, say, oh the kids, you know kids, the kids will be back by and by.

The inspector, we knew, was just doing his job.

A job was a job.

The number of kids you were registered for was the number of kids you were supposed to produce if someone asked. They could be small and clinging to your knees or big and looming from behind, but you were supposed to line them up to be counted for inspection. Counting was so easy anyone could do it: 1-2-3.

The inspector was there. You were as hapless as ever. And all I could do was sit like a lump on a log in the next room over and think about a pumpkin. Don't ask me why. 1 always hated Halloween, but not 2. 2 loved Halloween with his whole giant heart even if the best I could come up with for a costume was a sheet—for ghost—when what he really looked like was a tiny Ghoul of the Ku Klux Klan. Thinking of him out there looking menacing and hateful like that tied me up in knots you can't imagine.

Whereas 1 was all in for the pumpkins, the whole family trip to the farm with the patch where we wandered about for him to find the biggest one, hauling it back in a little cart, his pure joy. Later, he'd hover at your side while you carved it, sometimes taking his small hand in yours to guide with your big one, scooping the eyes, jagging the teeth. The scarier the better for 1.

3 was afraid of all jack-o-lanterns, scary or happy. The sweetest and kindest of all human beings, she worried the candles would burn their brains.

After Halloween comes winter. 3 never made it through winter. That's how things went.

I had to think of something, though, once the inspector asked. I just wish it wasn't a pumpkin.

A better thought I might have had: a lake with schools of small shimmering fish and us on a dock peering down at them, the expressions of amazement on 1-2-3's faces, our happiest day.

They live in the lake like that, they cried, but how can they breathe?

How can any of us breathe, I thought, but didn't say, because if you don't have anything nice to say, my mother always said.

There were so many things I could have thought about—the rocks that glowed fluorescent when you shined a black light on them to delight the children you claimed not to know anything about now, your flannel shirt we used to swaddle them when they were new, my hiking boots I should have worn to change the outcome. Once 3 was gone, we could have tried again, if not for what happened to my leg the first time. But you know what, my leg was not that bad. With only one of them for each of us, we could have made it if we took things slow and went at night.

Or you could, I thought, but didn't say, because what was the point in that?

Still at the door, the inspector persisted, I'm very certain you do know. Everyone knows what we mean when we say *children*, as if all he really meant was why aren't they in school when that's not what he meant at all.

But even then, I didn't limp out to your side to tell him what I knew about children—how not so long ago, they'd been so very small, with tiny button eyes and nails as thin and translucent as the membranes of eggs. It was a lot of work. We had to take care of their every little need—put their little socks on their little feet, brush their little teeth, nurse them in their sickbeds as long as we could. And weren't we happy then, the best time of our lives? We carried them on hips and swung them from their feet and every night they came to fill up the whole ocean of bed between us like a little pod of whales and we cradled them and hugged them and told them it's okay when, clearly, it was not.

Or this: how very brave 1-2 turned out to be when you bought them their own hiking boots and explained what they were for. Maybe if I told him that, the inspector would have trusted us, put his suspicions behind him, and not done the thing he did with the tag which was to attach it to the lobe of your ear where it hung not at all like an earring.

It wasn't my fault what happened to 3, and it wasn't yours either.

But oh, we could have used a little 4 right then. It wouldn't have had to be pretty, and it wouldn't have had to be smart or even good. All it would have had to be is small—and ours. One might have been enough.

The tag meant what it meant. We had three days. What can you do with three days? Roast a cauliflower, take a long ride on your bike, cross the ocean of your bed like in a boat—a lifeboat!

Now the inspector was gone and you stood there in the door still, the tag hanging down from your ear with a little bit of blood where it hooked into your skin.

Well, that's that, then, I thought. My leg is my leg. I'm not getting far on my leg, maybe not even as far as 1-2 got when you sent them away in their boots as if that might keep the inspectors at bay. After that, I didn't know what to think, what you were hoping to accomplish or how much bed between us we could take. People have their reasons, and you must have had yours.

Account R

The rule was: Each one, one—one serving of food, one cover for your bed, one shirt for your back, one memory, one dream, one confidante.

Not that we were parsimonious, per se. But there was only so much to go around.

The color (one) for the covers on our beds was blue, said to be a calming color, like sky or water. Were we calm?

We were steadfast. We were stalwart. That has to count for something.

My memory was a meadow. Not the kind of meadow you might think, with flowers and a gurgling brook, but swarming with mosquitos and sticky with late summer heat, and I was moving through it fast. On my back, I carried something heavy and, in my chest, a heavy feeling too. My feet—my whole body—hurt. It wasn't going to be long before this moving fast—either toward or away from whatever it was I was rushing toward or away from—was over, but for now, I kept on pushing through the meadow, not really running but not walking either, all sweaty and panting and slapping at mosquitoes and trying not to think about all the diseases they might carry.

What kind of memory was that?

Other people's memories were pleasing. One person had a memory of cookies, another had a memory of sex. All our memories were different, but you only got the one. You could sometimes trade them—you can have my memory of midnight for your memory of swimming—but most of the time, you got what you got. I got my meadow. It was hot and buggy. And who'd fucking want to trade me for that?

One person had a memory of punning, and in her dream we were each of us down to a single word. How sad is that?

If you only got one word, what word would that be? I'll tell you what my one word would not be, and that is "fucking," although I do see how it might be useful in all its fungibility.

Most of us tried not to feel that way—the wretchedness, the bitter despair. Why should we? The memory governed the dream and with it, your feelings. If your memory was pleasing, you could lie beneath your cover (blue) and wait for pleasing dreams, with your fine, benevolent feelings about the rest of us.

The thing about the confidantes, you couldn't really call them friends. You were allowed to tell them things— you could pour your heart out—but whoever was your confidante, you were never theirs. You'd tell them things and, what, would they turn around and tell your things to their confidante? Were we all dreaming the same dream?

One day my confidante got to telling me about the way things used to be. I listened because listening was my job, but it seemed like a transgression, for even if she claimed her memory was "the past," how could it hold so many things and what was I supposed to do with glut like that—one lover for the daytime and another for the night, meals with all kinds of food groups in them, different shoes for inside and for outside, rainbow-colored blankets. By the time she finished, a sinking feeling had come over me and all I wanted was to sleep.

After we parted, I thought about the person whose memory was cookies and dream was working in a bakery. If that were my dream, I told myself, what I'd think about all day would be the children. They wouldn't be children like the ones in the time my confidante told me about who could have all the treats they wanted and playdates galore—everything changes, you know—but they would still be children who'd come in after school clutching tokens for their cookies, the looks on their faces, when the baking smell washed over them, what we once might have called rapt—or rapturous?

I wonder about that.

And then I wonder, when the children would come in, rapt or rapturous, what kind of baker would I be? Would I make them open their grubby, little hands to reveal the tokens inside? Would I poke them with my finger and count the tokens one by one? Would I send them away if the tokens were short?

Or would I instead welcome the children with a smile as warm as a mother's hug once and set out the cookies on platters and never count tokens at all?

You could probably get away with this if you set out broken cookies. We used to feed broken cookies to dogs (if your memory included dogs). But what else could you get away with if you were like my confidante and broke the rules?

That night I lay beneath my cover (blue) and slapped mosquitoes in my sleep. I knew about mosquitoes, but I didn't know why my memory was of them. A meadow is generally a pleasing thing, with flowers, so why was mine swarming with bugs?

Why, oh why, oh why? Oh, what a hideous riddle.

In my one dream, I am rushing, always rushing toward or away from something—*toward* or *away*—but when I tell my confidante this, my confidante says, it has to be one or the other, it cannot be both.

Account B

We came home from a walk in the woods and found something waiting for us. It wasn't a this, or a that, or a they; it was a *bunch*. Bunches were soft and changed colors when you petted them—little spots of turquoise turning tangerine, chartreuse to celadon, lilac to lime. And if you put your ear up close, they purred. But this new bunch just sat there like a garden gnome or tortoise, its overall color so nondescript we might have missed it if it weren't hunkered down in the middle of our welcome mat. The bunch wasn't that big, but it was plenty big enough for us to have to step around it to go through our front door.

Oh brother, you said, now what?

Don't worry, I said. Let me think.

The last time we had some bunches around they took to sleeping here and there—at the back of the bread box, under the yarn in your basket, between my rolled socks. They weren't so much trouble back then, but they were messy. Whatever went into the bunches came out. That's in the nature of things.

The next thing you said was something about how much bigger this bunch was than our last bunch of bunches. It wasn't going to be able to nest neatly among our piles of shoes or between our yeasty loaves of bread, but there it was, before our door, and if we let it in, it would have to go somewhere.

Bunches don't come in just ones, you said. No one ends up with only one bunch.

We stood on our porch regarding the bunch and remembering how nice it had been on our walk in the woods among the tall trees with the blue sky above, the wind like a breath that blew all our troubles away. Now we were home. I knew and you knew—we both knew—you were right. One bunch wasn't so bad. Even a big bunch like this one, you could work around it or shove it aside with your boot, but sweet as its little purr was, a whole bunch of bunches this big would soon make a great racket. Remembering my fondness for sleep, I sighed.

But what to do?

You weren't supposed to harbor bunches. Before, okay, a bunch or two, no problem. Children liked to pet them and make their colors turn, and despite their messiness, they could be useful. If you rolled them around on a shelf or the floor, they cleaned up your messes along with their own. They could lull you to sleep with a gentle whooshing noise from underneath your bed. They had a fondness for ants. But after what happened before, no more. You find a bunch, you call it in. That was the rule.

We stood there for a while, ruefully regarding the bunch.

I'm going to call it in, you said at last.

And then we let your words hang between us for another furtive while, until I said no, don't.

We didn't want to know what happened to the bunches after people called them in. Whatever it was, it was sure to be unpleasant. We knew this from before when if you stepped on one by accident (and really, who could help it?), the sound it made was more a squeal than squeak. There's a big difference between a squeal and a squeak, even if it's only one letter. Thinking this now, such a quietness fell over us that even the bunch shut off. Back when our little house was full of them, a connection grew among us, for certainly—it's hard to know quite how to say this—they had a kind of *companionability*, not unlike the one shared between you and me. In addition to their purring, the soft parts of them were so very, very *soft*—every bit as soft as the softest parts of us.

What I'm trying to say is, standing there back from our walk in the woods and faced with this oversized bunch on our porch, we didn't quite know what to do. It was not supposed to be there, but it was. The sun was going down, and in the air, a chill was rising. Despite the rules, we wanted to go in, for our troubles blown away by the wind in the woods were beginning to gather behind us again, and I couldn't help but wonder what would happen if I stooped down to pick up the bunch and took it inside with us.

What, for that matter, if you did?

Account P

Prescience came to all of us in time. You couldn't stop it. I couldn't stop it. No one could, not that we didn't try. There was plenty of doom to go around as things were, why invite more from the future?

No one started out with it, of course. We had rosebuds for cheeks and buttons for toes, like anyone else. They kept us like that for as long as they could. It was the least they could do.

Then they put us in rooms and waited to see what would develop. Your room was the color of milk; my room was the color of thick. What color is thick, you might ask, but you don't want to know.

We each had our room now, both you and me, but we were waiting too. That's what the rooms were for.

What I miss about the time before they put us in our rooms is a word that will not do it justice, which is bedlam. The meaning of bedlam is uproar and confusion, although it also once referred to institutions for the mentally insane.

We are not insane; we are prescient instead.

For some of us, prescience goes both ways—forwards into the future, backwards into the past.

Before the rooms, we rolled around on the floor all together in one great chamber and slurped our gruel from one shared bowl; we slept side-by-side in a long row of beds pushed so close together we could reach out and hold hands in the spaces between. In this way, we learned we are connected and sowed the seeds of our dedication and our purpose.

After the rooms, no more bedlam. Developing took time. It could be lonely at first. But between your milk-colored room and my thick-colored one, a crack—or hole—they hadn't filled. Sometimes, through the hole, I could hear you breathing. You breathed with a rasp in your throat that smelled green. Sometimes, I tried breathing back. It was the best I could do.

Then, as our prescience came, either with a wallop or in dribs and drabs, our breathing changed. For you, a little sour; for me, who can smell their own breath? Wallops were hard enough, but dribs and drabs could also take their toll. Oh no, we'd think, but then we couldn't quite say what had alarmed us, or we'd suddenly be crumpled in tears on the floor. Backwards prescience, the rarest of all, came with a stab of regret, as useless as it was uncommon. Included in it was everything—*everything*—that had gone on before. We called this memory, but what were we supposed to do with all the things in it—shove them under the bed? The joys of bedlam notwithstanding, you couldn't change a stitch about the past. Whereas the true value of prescience: anticipation, mitigation, salvation. Compared to all of that, what earthly good was hindsight?

For most of us, prescience started with a dream. We'd wake up, a cry on our lips as if from another language or world. There was no stopping it now. Once you had one dream, more were coming. Our dreams were like windows to the future. Prophesy, they told us, is a gift.

The way to tell the difference between the future and the past is, one, you wake up with a clutch at your heart, the other, a stab of remorse.

In addition to the colors of our rooms, they contained, as well, our traits. Your trait was wholesome, mine was bulwark; I was the finger in the dike, you were the surge of the sea. At night, we breathed our dreams to each other. I was holding things off as long as I could, but you were all come-what-may, as if that might soften the outcome.

After the rooms came windows. That's where they took us when we were ready. We were supposed to tell what we saw.

It's not no color, you prophesied, but it's close, a kind of dun.

When you said that, I knew your time was coming, but I still kept on shoving memories under my bed from the time when the world was the color of root. My root-colored world was chock full of things and your dun-colored one was what you called empty—no trees, you said, with a catch in your breath. No shade for the people, no beds for their sleep.

The others lay in their rooms, the cries from their dreams caught on their lips, but we bided the time as best we could as I tried to impart my gift of common memory to you.

Oh, we said through the hole in our wall. Oh, we said. Oh, we said: *oh!*

The uselessness of hindsight is: Don't cry over spilt milk.

But the future grows out of the past, and this knowledge has a smell to it like the mattress you slept on or the shoes we once wore fashioned from beautiful animals with many stomachs and wet, brown eyes and something called cud. We didn't think about what happened to the animals when we wore them on our feet. It was enough to think cud.

Looking back, it's clear to me you had a holy circuit for your dreams while all I ever had was a dogged purpose. You were going to save us from the future, but all I could do was fret about the past. Thinking that, I better understand how bedlam was never the right word. In the vast communion we once shared, all of us together, maybe there was uproar and confusion, but there was also skin and frolic, even if we were just rosebuds and buttons. You need to be precise about your words if you want to stay in your room with your dreams which, like it or not, is better than where you are going to go once they decide you are ready.

The word I choose is love. I nab it and use it because it is precisely what I mean—I *loved* our time together in our rooms, I *loved* the breath that passed between us through the hole we shared, I *loved* you. Sometimes, through the hole, all I heard was breathing. *Your* breathing, I thought. Then I closed my eyes, and this is what I saw: not a glass of milk or piece of pie, not a button or a bud, but a pasture and a barn. The pasture had creatures in it with snouts in the grass to fill up their multiple stomachs. Inside the barn, more creatures with cud being milked.

I *love* milk. Don't you?

Before they took you away, we whispered through the hole all night until our tongues got hot and swollen because we both knew what was coming. Everyone has a job to do, they said, when all they really wanted was to know what happens next.

Another word for room is fortress.

You breathe in, I breathe out. That is the most we can do.

When I think about your room now, I think of all the words I know, but none are what I mean.

The wall was too massive to shove anything through, only our voices. That is the nature of fortresses. But you could blow your breath through it into my ear. When you blew into my ear, this is what I heard: wind. Also, things like rain and cymbals and what you'd be afraid of when they took you to your window for your final view. You were afraid if it was low, things would be too close; you were afraid if it was high, you would see too far. You were afraid it would hurt.

Because you didn't know how gentle the sound of rain could be, you were afraid of that too.

Be afraid of missing me, I wanted to blow back into your ear, but in the absence of human memory, once you were gone, you were going to be gone, so what I did instead was this: I crawled under my bed and blew everything I'd stashed there as hard as I could through the hole in our wall back to you.

Account S

A man came into town. He was walking down the road in a pair of rubber sandals. He had walked all the way from the low range of mountains to the west, past the yellow lake, through the old mining center, to the edge of our town where the orange trees grew. It was a long way to walk. In his hands, he was carrying something that had once been alive. He had white hair. Some of his teeth were missing. When he breathed, soft wheezing came out of his chest, hollow and flute-like. What he was carrying, his final possession, he was bringing to us.

Oh dear, one of us said. Why us?

This is what comes, another said, from hiding out in the hills. He can blame himself.

And at once, we all agreed, putting our uneasiness aside and imputing the man in our hardest of hearts for what had happened to him and the something he was carrying when why didn't he come to us sooner? There he stood in the road, furtively eyeing the men in our trees whose gunlines were sighted on him and not so certain now what to do now with the something still cradled in his arms. Almost, he seemed to want to hold it out to us, but too late is too late, we thought, not without some righteous vindication.

After a while, he knelt and laid it gently in the road.

And then, without a word, he turned to start his long trek back into the hills.

Later, a woman among us commenced having visions that had nothing to do, she said, with what was going on in the mountains to the west but only right there in our town with the food we ate, the blankets we wrapped ourselves in, and the stories we told our children about what we had done when we were like the man who had come to us out of the mountains bearing his something—living or not—to ensure they had oranges to eat.

Notice, she said, the whiteness of his hair. Is our hair white? she said. No, it is not.

One of the children had rolled him an orange. And that's when the visions began.

Also, she told us, a spaceship was coming. It was going to be round and as white as that man's hair or our memories of snow. It would make no sound, be luminous, and float like the bubbles we made to amuse the children who were, but for the one who rolled the orange, obedient and neat.

And you know, it was harder to believe in the things that happened here when we were like the man in rubber sandals who had walked so far to bring us his something, living or not, than it was to believe in the spaceship that was coming, round and white and hopeful, like us. If we still believed in writing, that's what we would write. We would write about the aliens inside. That's what hope is like. It's like writing.

But the spaceship, when it came, was certainly not white. We could see it though, no real color we had ever known and hovering for days above the low range of mountains where the man had emerged to bring us his something that might still have been alive when he started out, although surely it was not when he left it on the road. We stood there, in our sensible shoes and our firm belief in orange juice, not judging him, really, but not not judging him either. So he left it on the road, and we left it there too. Who would want it now?

The child who rolled him an orange was punished, that was for sure—as if we had oranges to spare!

One day we looked out and the thing was gone, taken away in the night by whatever it is that takes such things away in the night when no one is watching. We all sighed a collective sigh more of relief than remorse because that's what we're like.

Some time after that, the spaceship came, just as the woman had foreseen.

But even though we knew, because she'd told us, what was going to happen, we knew she was wrong, and the wrongness was not what we, or our children, were going to do the next time a man brought us something—living or not—but what we had already done, for as long and as hard as we could, to harvest the oranges, fragrant and sweet, that grew along the borders of our town and to squeeze them for our children for the juice that would keep them strong and optimistic, like us, in the town where such wondrous things grew. We knew this even as we watched the spaceship that was no color at all and had nothing to do with writing as it drifted away from the low range of mountains where the man started out and where it had hovered for days.

What were we to do but watch? That's where the spaceship had landed.

Not here.

Account P2

There should have been something different about the rock.

Too round, some said.

Too yellow, others mused.

Still others remarked on its lack of porosity, for it was full of holes, like pumice, but impervious to liquid, taking only what it seemed to want.

Observing this, we did our best to keep both our distance and suspicions to ourselves. Why stir things up when things were plenty stirred up enough? And why would such a rock—this unnatural rock—appear one day where before there had been no rock on the site of the last remaining portal?

Despite our better judgment, a grumbling spread among us that soon included whispered confabs over coffee, schoolyard altercations, stony lunchroom silences, and late-night ruminations between lovers (who, despite all odds, persisted) until finally we agreed to convene.

We convened in the square that had once been a park at the location of the last remaining portal. Ringing the square, a few rows of trees from which still fell the small, yellow flowers of the vine that had crept all the way to the crowns of the trees, seeking the last of the sun. The yellow of the flowers was more brilliant than the yellow of the rock, but both were the color of light. Beyond the square, rows of tall apartment buildings in which lay the beds of the persistent lovers (but not the lovers, who were gathered with us here) and, on the street below, the coffeehouse tables where earlier that morning we had sat and squabbled over our few remaining ideas. If you looked, that was all you could see, but none of us were looking. We were looking at the rock.

When the portal had been open, you could lose things through it, sure. Some of the things we knew for certain we had lost: all bathroom scales (although no one was fat anymore), music stands and clarinets and armatures and strings (because musicians were the first to go out in the somberness of the historical moment that had wiped out even the memory of the human voice singing), pastries and poodles and cats and dogs and parrots and most boys and girls.

Also missing: all that had once lain beyond the square where we were gathered at the site of the last remaining portal and, now, its yellow rock. Everyone knew this, some from the gossip that still swirled through the coffeehouse and beds of the persistent lovers, but others from what they had seen when they had gone out to look for themselves, although what they had seen had been hard to describe.

You could only go so far walking down the streets until the streets—they didn't know what to call it—somehow petered out. Well, that's what some said. Others said you walked for a while, maybe five or six blocks, and then all that happened was you came to the end. This is what the end looked like: a blank wall, swirling space, sand.

Around the square, we faced each other, the rock firmly anchored at our center. Some of us clutched coffee mugs and others the hands of our persistent lovers. The rock could not be budged—we had tried. It would be part of us now forever. There wasn't so much that remained, but all that remained was there, where we were, and by the time we convened we had begun to understand this. The portals had all been so efficient, everything gone down them—*gone, gone.*

A child—the last child—spoke first. Now what are we going to do?

From beneath the rock a low thrumming sound began, like a sigh, or SOS, or exultation.

Everyone thought about what had been taken from us.

And that's how we started, with the memories of things—all the things we'd lost—and why, *oh why,* hadn't we done more to safeguard them?

Account P3

That was the day the parachute-thing appeared in the sky without a bundle or a man hanging from it, just a tangle of straps below and a flaccid blue parachute-thing above. Or it could have been orange—it's hard to recall.

Well, someone said, ahem.

Let's not get carried away, another said.

Someone else made the sound of a long, low whistle.

Without a bundle or a man hanging from it, the parachute-thing floated in the sky, a great blue or orange tarpaulin adrift on the wind but with a seeming purpose—or *direction*—now hovering over the one-legged woman who lived in the hut at the end of the lane, now over the man with pocked jowls and a paunch who'd run what was once our mini-golf course, now over the tree that was losing its leaves for the last time on earth, now over you, now over me.

Torn between dread and desire, we wondered who was next.

The tangle of straps dangling from the parachute-thing hung there all floppy and loose, as if once it might have held a bundle or a man. The straps seemed okay—not frayed or worn—but they weren't buckled either.

I wonder what that means, someone said.

Don't say that, another reproved.

No one wanted to think about what happened to the bundle or the man that had once been buckled in but now was not. If it was a bundle, had it been for us? If a man, what news had he been bringing? Either way, somewhere a splat-thing—bundle or man—lay on the ground. Who'd want to think about that?

Next day, same thing—the giant quivering blue or orange floating thing above us, us looking up at it wondering.

And the next after that, and the next.

After a while, most of the others started to act like it was normal to have a thing like that happen. The one-legged woman and the pock-jowled man carried on as if they shared a common secret; you could see them sometimes conferring—or *conspiring*—underneath their eaves. They seemed to *like* it. Whereas you and I, we started thinking things we never would have thought before: What happened to the other leg, what's with all those pockmarks? There was a kind of hard and edgy bitterness, I mean.

Until even I began to harbor suspicions: What good could come from a parachute-thing that neither descended all the way to the ground nor drifted away somewhere else? Not to mention the splat thing. Which you had to wonder: Either man or bundle, was it a harbinger to tell us rules had changed? And if the rules had changed, did we still live in the right, as was our purpose and our wont, or were we now transgressors without warning?

All this made our heads hurt, but no matter how hard we tried, we could not stop thinking of the man or bundle now unloosed such that soon we began to stay inside our little house so as not to have to see the floating thing above us or think about what it might portend. Inside, we tried to be kind, hiding love notes for each other and making both sides of the bed just because. Inside, it was almost okay. But no, not quite, because of our shared, unspoken thought that it could also be a woman.

One night, we decided we'd had enough and went out for a walk. First, we walked all the way to the tree that used to bear some kind of fruit where, when we were young, you carved our names with an arrow sticking through them but forgot the heart. Then we strolled past the old mini-golf course where the man who used to run it littered little twigs and acorns around the last hole so no one would win a free game, except one time you did. Finally, we made our way to the central square where we sat on a bench and thought some thoughts until your head drifted down to my shoulder and you took my hand in yours and sighed. Bundle, man—or woman—perhaps we'd never know, but what if the splat thing were not entirely splat? And what about the animals out there, who were also hungry?

By now the parachute-thing was no longer either blue or orange but a blanched and blotchy dun, and sometimes when it hovered over us, we could see things in the blotches the way we used to see things in the clouds—a tiny dog with a ruff of glowing feathers; the word COW; petunias, peppermints, and pantaloons. Everything we saw, we had a name for. And even though sometimes you saw one thing and sometimes I saw another, the names we had for what we saw would still suffice, until, one day, they did not. One day we looked up and saw something we didn't know what to call it.

We tried a bunch of words we knew that, even if they weren't quite right, we hoped were good enough: axolotl, winklepicker, snowplow.

Oh, oh, oh.

Milk, turmeric, sassafras.

When I said God, you said, no! Then you added, a bit more gently, at least take the capital off.

But lower case or upper didn't make us feel any better or change a single thing about our destiny. Because the one word we couldn't bring ourselves to say and never would again was *future*—even though that is precisely what the blotch looked like, and we both knew it.

It's funny, though, what people can get used to. People can get used to a lot.

And so, at last the morning came when, despite not really wanting to, you packed your little backpack, and I packed mine. You checked the stove, and I checked the iron, and we both checked the windows and doors and turned off the lights, and then all that we owned in the world secured, we went out to search for whatever it was that was going to turn out to be what we found, which began, in the way of all such journeys, with us walking down the road, the only road we had. We just picked a direction and took it, first you, then me.

It's hard to say quite how we felt about that. Home, after all, is home, and sure we were going to miss it. Everything that was going to happen until we came back (or not) would already be done by then. But our feet knew better than our hearts, and it wasn't long before we'd walked away from everything we knew and loved and found ourselves in an open countryside of rolling hills and yellow grasses and maybe somewhere in them whatever was left of the splat-thing after all this time. We didn't say much as we walked, there not being much to say. We'd both packed enough to last a long time but hoped it wouldn't come to that. We hoped we'd find it right away and be home in time for supper.

People hope the things they hope. You can't do much about that.

Our first night out, you laid your mat under a stone outcropping to be sheltered from the open sky, and I laid mine in a meadow by a little stream to look up at the stars in it, the gauzy Milky Way. Then we wrapped ourselves tight as cocoons and slept the sleep of the righteous, for old rules or new ones, we were still pretty sure about that.

But we hadn't gone very far the next morning before something made you stiffen up and look back, so I did too. Behind us lay our town. We'd climbed enough already to have a bit of a view but were still close enough to make out the remains of our mini-golf course and the tendrils of smoke curling out of the chimneys, the bright morning light glinting off all the east-facing windows. It should have tugged at our heartstrings a bit, except—what was the parachute thing doing way out there?

Is that all we've walked, you muttered.

What, I tried not to say, is it *following* us?

Looking down on the distance we had covered, it was clear to see that while the parachute-thing was still closer to town than to us, it had somehow drifted farther than it ever had before. Before, it had always seemed somehow tethered to our central square and had never even gotten as far as the church at the top of the hill at the edge of town and surely not the graveyard where everyone was buried for countless generations. Now it was there.

Which is precisely why we didn't want to think the very next thing we thought: *oh, brother*, what happens if the tether, like the harness, snaps?

The end, you didn't say but we both felt it, like something blowing in and entirely through us: *the end, the end*.

Beyond the town a field lay. In the field, a barn.

If it gets as far as the barn, you said.

Whereas I, I said nothing at all, for what was there left to say?

We walked another three days, each day the same, until there was no denying the parachute thing was drifting a little bit farther from town, a little bit closer to us.

That night—our last night on earth—we placed our mats side-by-side in a meadow and lay down together beneath the stars, thinking our thoughts. The stars were far away and beautiful and, among them, other planets, not unlike our own. We loved the sparkle of those stars every bit as much as we loved the stars themselves and held them in our hearts with a kind of marvel, but the planets stirred something different in us.

Home, we thought, neither one of us wanting to sleep.

So you took my hand in yours and sang a little song I'd never heard before, and I sang a little song I never knew I'd known, and then we couldn't stop singing back and forth from me to you until we'd been singing for so long we could hardly keep it up, but still we continued with a gentle humming until, unable to put it off anymore, and just before drifting finally to sleep, you rolled to your side and mumbled—part song, part speech—almost as if to yourself from a dream, I wonder where they put it.

Put what? I murmured.

The moon, you said. The *moon*.

And when we woke up, there it was!—the parachute-thing but purged of its blotches, just a great, white luminescent orb shimmering in the morning sun with a kind of milky glow and hovering there above us every bit as moon-like as if we were a planet of our own. And isn't that an odd thing? In the darkness of our hearts, all along we had been thinking we were looking for the splat-thing, when instead the parachute-thing had been looking for us!

We weren't singing anymore, but why not?

Oh, what a beautiful morning, we might well have sung.

This is going to take some getting used to, we both thought, but we didn't have much time because even as we thought this, the parachute-thing did the other thing it had never done before, beginning its descent and billowing in the wind like any other normal parachute as it drifted *down, down, down* until it was close enough at last to lower its harness to us on Earth.

Account P4

Of course, there will be animals, although we might not recognize them.

With irregular limbs growing out of wrong places—from the orifice of ears, for example, or between the toes—they may have membranes where eyes used to be, or humps where there once were long elegant necks. And while it's unclear what will remain of their voice boxes, surely, they'll make some kind of sounds. But what kind of sounds will they be?

Should we fear them, these animals of the postworld?

Oh, naturally, some. For like those of today, some will feed on others, including those that feed on us, should we share this planet with them, which we will not.

What would we have named them, I wonder?

Nonetheless, I, for one, have fallen haplessly in love with their dark opacities and chalky luminescences, and it's hard not to long for a time we could have shared together, galloping along on shaggy, nine-legged creatures across vast deserts of glowing rock. Impossible to say how we know these rocks will glow, but glow they will as, large and small and all over the planet, they settle into vacant cavities where houses once stood.

Some things, of course, will not change—geology, for example, and water, which will still go in cycles, although how long will these cycles be? Ice may linger for what we once called millennia, or steam may envelop the planet, eliminating distinctions between rain and not rain.

Love?

Most emphatically, yes. Rocks will lodge against each other, faithful forever and glowing as rocks will glow then; so too the steadfast lap of waves, which will continue long after our world does not.

Also, in some of the parts of the postworld, most vicious of all will be plants. Gigantic or microscopic, they'll go after one another with raw colonizing greed we'd find woefully familiar, were we here. Don't assume the big ones will prevail either.

Wonder, instead, about the color of the sky, what the earth will taste like, how the wind will speak when we are gone.

Part 2

Mewl

And meanwhile, another day, how dreadful, another day, how fortunate.

—Javier Marías

I found out from a postcard slipped underneath our door. On the postcard was a screenshot, on the screenshot was a map, or something like it. But it wasn't an ordinary map, and I knew if I showed you, you'd say something smug, like *ha! the interregnum*, but the interregnum wasn't any kind of place, it was a kind of time, and we were in it. The more I studied the map, the less sense it made, just a bunch of squiggly lines with a red mark in the center and on the mark, a word, but who could read a word like that? I didn't know anything else—if it was an invitation or a warning or an edict or a conclave or what planet it was even on (you had your theories, I had mine), but I knew— *oh didn't I!*—I wanted to be there.

Then I found out you already knew.

What, were you hiding it from me?

But because I understood you really were trying to protect me and who had room for anger anymore, I decided to ignore it. If we pooled our resources, meager as they were, just imagine what if.

So I kept on studying my postcard and you kept on trudging up the hill to the market where the few remaining stragglers were still spreading useless information. There weren't enough left to count as a convening, one or two among the aisles with nothing on the shelves or hunkered down on the stools where we used to order coffee with milk made of nuts from all over the world, but whether it was an uprising or a powwow or a ship, who could say? All they could say was go alone, take a partner, no children, only children (a *children's crusade!*), bring something of value to trade—trail mix, socks, a flute. But what good was information like that when what we really needed was a legend for my map?

Except, okay, maybe not.

Because it might be a trick! We weren't spring chickens anymore, what if one of us got hurt? And what, neither one of us liked to think, were we supposed to do about the girl?

So one day you were for it—*let's go, let's go!* The next, my turn. Back and forth, pro and con. It got so heated up between us that I sometimes thought did we really want to be the kind of people who one day in the distant future would have to look back on all that had happened since and see ourselves as the first to rush out, flailing our arms like everyone else—*take us!*

Didn't we used to be better than that?

And what about the boys?

What boys? you said. I thought you said girl, because you were stubborn like that.

We argued about when to go.

We argued about how.

I said, motorcycle.

You said, boat.

My motorcycle went fast, but your boat could float.

My motorcycle had red racing stripes.

Your boat had blue oars.

Heading down a river in the silent swish of night would have been swell. I loved your boat, I really did. I loved the things we'd see in it and how it smelled of everywhere—the sea, the marsh, the barest whiff of the late idea of a parent cruise. Sometimes it even smelled of parents, dry as martinis and gruff as dads. My motorcycle stank of the last gasp of fossil fuel. Who could love a scent like that? But it could climb mountains and roar *vroom-vroom*. Your boat was nice, no question, but if we put the pedal to the metal, imagine how far we could go on my bike before anyone knew we were gone!

Seas were wild and free, you said, and if we took a boat, we could maybe hook up with a cruise. The cruises weren't for people like us, but if we showed up in a little boat, would they really be so heartless as to barge on over us and leave us in their wake? Mountains had caves for hiding and overlooks for standing watch on everything coming at us.

Things weren't urgent yet, but they were getting there, and in all the hoopla, sometimes we almost forgot about the girl, but then we'd stumble over her little nest of pillows on the floor, and she'd leap up out of them, jabbering and waving her hands at us to fire up the blank parts at the center of our brains until all that was left was the rue of them.

I missed the mewling, didn't you? Things hadn't been so bad when all she did was mewl.

In the end, because we know there's never going to be either boat or motorcycle, we walk. It's easy. First, we gather our things to set out by the front door, like a suitcase or a go-bag, but without much purpose to it, just stuffing this thing and that thing—changes of underwear, legumes, something to write all this down—into the little sacks I made to carry on our backs without thinking very much about what it is for or what else we are going to need and with a hapless feeling tugging at our tired, old wormy hearts: What if someone—I'm not saying who—comes back to find animals in our sweet little house, not us? And then we sleep on it one last night, our last remaining dream passing from you to me and back again until we can't tell which one of us took flight like what once was a bird and which plunged off the bluff into a deep, blue body of water when nothing is blue or deep anymore.

In the morning, we wake up in a thrall of apprehension, brush our teeth one last time with our memory of mint, and meet at our front door, our guardian and savior all this time.

Well, you say.

And I just nod and gulp.

But before my slew of second thoughts can gather up the sense to cry, *no, wait!* the girl is already open and out, flooding our little entryway with a rush of outside air that feels every bit as sharp and dangerous as I was afraid it would. Anything could happen in it, anything at all. But too late now. What can we do but follow the girl, planting our feet one after the other until we end up where we have to go and find out the truth of this planet where we have lived out the interregnum and lost even the memory of our two boys?

So that's how we start, walking down the road as if it's the most natural thing in the world, the girl first, then you, then me. Except for the ash and the leaves here and there that drift through the air without ever reaching the ground, things seem pretty much the same, only a little bit different. Inside the houses, animals watch us go, paws at the windows, tongues slack in their jaws, but are their eyes soft and friendly or vicious and snarly? Do they smell sour and rank, or of a strange and earthy musk we wish we might have known?

Did you lock the door, I say.

Did you check the stove?

After that, we don't say anything at all, the two of us walking along behind the girl with our heads held up as high as they go on what sure seems like Earth. At least I *hope* so! Because now that we're out, I feel such a surge of affection for it all—the trees on our street, the rocks in the ground, the very ground itself—don't you? The trees stand where they stand, and we pass by, moving through time as much as space, each moment falling behind us and not coming back until finally I put one of my hands in one of yours and the other one into my pocket where, at the last minute, I'd slipped my old phone. Don't ask me why. All the people who pop up in it are strangers to us now when once we surely loved them, whether or not they texted back.

What would happen if I fired up my phone?

No, you say, don't.

And of course, you are right. For the charge on this phone in my pocket might well be the last charge on Earth—or wherever we are—and when it is gone, the mysteries of the people and the world it contains will be gone too.

Then the girl turns back with a look on her face we can't parse and says something that sounds like *kmwgb gtyug xxzcdq* or else, don't worry. It's hard to tell.

But we're on our way now, so what does it matter, even if the farther we walk from our sweet little house, the stronger the blank part in the center of our brains fires up with something sad missing from it. And as soon as I think that—*that exact moment*—a subtle shift between us—not so much a sudden doubt as a kind of recognition—and then, from the one to the other, a single sighed *mewl*. There's no immediate danger, at least not yet, so okay, humor her. What's gone is gone.

But I still stop to write *please call me* in the ash on the hood of a car.

And on others, you write the number for my phone, just in case.

What are we even hoping for anyway—boys who aren't boys anymore, everything we've lost? You've lost it, too, don't get me wrong, you who thought the best thing in the world would be to hole up in the hills and rescue stray girls like cats. Just don't think about it, you always said, as if one day all this would pass and things would be normal again, like normal was something to hope for.

I'll tell you what passes—life passes. You start out small and sweet like everyone; then you're old and hoary and there's a smell to you that isn't nice at all. This all happens in what seems like a blink. You think you might escape all the indignity, and then you hope you won't. This last thought is not terribly useful, but I have it anyway because we're not in some distant future looking back on something we can't remember that couldn't possibly have happened, we're stuck in the raveling present which we can't escape and in which we have left our sweet little house in the hills to take off for who knows where because someone shoved a postcard with a screenshot through our door and because there is a time for everything, and this is it.

The only thing we wish we brought more of is socks.

We walked for a while. We walked a bit more. We walked until I had a pain in my side and you had a gimp in your limp, and none of the places we walked through reminded us of anything, not even the dentist.

After that, we kept on walking, as if walking was all that was left in the world and we would keep doing it forever or at least until we got there, whichever came first. In time, the houses thinned out, then dropped off behind us, with maybe an outlying barn or two far in the distance or an abandoned gas station at the side of the road until there was nothing left of them either and the road turned to dirt at our feet with a few spiky plants we might once have known the names of. Something about the bright yellow flowers bursting out of their papery stalks at least seemed familiar, but then, in vague ways, they did not. Seeing that whatever we'd packed in our sacks was not going to do us much good way out here, the rest of our brains went as blank as the spots at their centers and we stopped thinking much of anything at all. We didn't think water or food or how much farther is it going to be. We didn't think parents or hiking sticks. We didn't think sweet little house or bird thump or boys or not-boys, *poof*, our minds as empty and porous as sieves and, after a while, a kind of peaceful feeling settling into them when suddenly, with no warning, the girl stepped off the road ahead and started to bushwhack it off in no real direction at all.

Now what?

A hush fell over the world then, leaving us more alone than ever—no swoosh of bird, nor wind, nor breath, nor even footfalls of the girl as she pressed on ahead, with or without us.

What happened next is hard to explain.

After we stepped off the road, the air still smelled like air and the ground was still rocky beneath our feet and the plants still grew from it here and there, but you have to admit, fewer and fewer. Other than that, not much. I don't know how to tell you what the blankness of this world was like, more like a smudge left behind by a dirty eraser than anything we ever might have cherished. And in the blur of sameness, earth dissolved into sky, sky into earth, and then nothing at all anymore as even the last few spiky plants fell off behind us.

Until out of the nothing—I'm not kidding—a great tree appeared in the distance. And we had a name for it, and the name was oak. How is that even possible, when didn't all the great oaks die in the blight? But there it was before us, the last living oak on the planet and, all around it, the unbounded emptiness of a world stripped bare of everything lovely while you and I were hiding out in our sweet little house hoping things might change without us. It looked like shelter and, sure, we were going to need it—if only the girl would slow down ahead, maybe we could catch up and rest. How long have we been walking anyway? We're not so young, you know.

But no—and this is the part, well, don't ask me how—when we stopped to call out, *hey wait*, she'd already disappeared around some kind of bend. I know what you're thinking. You're thinking: How could there be a bend in all this nothing? But you don't say it because it's not going to be long now before we disappear around it too.

So that's what happened: *Whoosh*!

Around the bend was something.

The something, I don't know what to call it.

A structure? But what kind of structure could it be, patchworked in a crazyquilt of something like wood—but very old wood, wood old enough to have lain on a beach for a thousand years and under the ground for a thousand more until it turned into a kind of stone or shell, the fossilized lines of its plates like a map—*my* map! But whether the wood was already old when the structure was built or the structure itself had aged like that was impossible to tell. Otherwise, it made no sense. How could wood bend like that? What supported those spires? And here was another odd thing: Lacking any apparent mechanism to hold the structure together, its long, impossible slats of something like wood seemed to hover side-by-side with small gaps between to let air or light in—or out—and bend in an endless arc as vast and as round as a moon that curved in the distance into a horizon of its own. You could walk around it, maybe, but how long would that take? Days certainly, weeks, what remained of our lifetimes.

Or you could walk through it.

But there weren't any windows and just the one door.

Portal, you corrected me, wondering if there might not be another one on the other side. But we both knew there was not.

It's very dark in there, you said.

Don't you see, I said, how dark it is out here?

Before us, the girl stood facing the structure with one of her feet propped up on the shin of the opposite leg, like a bird somewhere between flight and sleep. And now, at last, I saw what you meant—she *did* remind me of someone, *oh yes*! But how could we ever find out who if we didn't turn back now and, I don't know, shelter for the night beneath the canopy of oak somehow already behind us, as if, in the morning, we might retrace our steps to our sweet little house and find everything waiting for us just as we'd left it, whether or not we'd checked the stove or locked the door. But when I tuned back, the tree was gone, disappeared behind the very same bend that had delivered us here—and in its place, well, nothing. Like everywhere else.

No, wait, I said, even as the girl turned to face us, arms akimbo, as if to say, what—thanks for everything, *ta-ta*, so long, you two, old doddering fools?

And then she said her final words to us, *bon voyage*.

Not that, I said, oh please, not yet.

But already she'd flipped herself upside down, hands on the ground and feet in the air as she went the way of the oak, twirling what looked like a hiking stick in her toes. And my heart leapt into my throat, but no, there you stood beside me, solid as a rock and every bit as stalwart as if we truly were in this together forever and ever, just you and just me the way you wanted, with the girl returned to wherever she came from and us on our own all over again.

So that's how we found ourselves here at last, where absent of tree and everything else, the earth at our feet— the exact same color as the sky at our heads—erased the difference between up and down, and the air tasted as much of the inside of something as it did of the outside.

Only the structure offered any dimension to what sure felt like a place that was nowhere.

I don't know how long we stood there studying the structure, grown suddenly old.

It could have been ages or half a human heartbeat. Finally, in my head, I heard a voice—a thin, reedy voice, or maybe two, with a bit of a lisp and something familiar to it. Just walk right into it, it said, without even having to add, please, or hurry up now, it's time. You must have heard it too because that's what we did. You took me by the hand as firmly and as warmly as if our lives lay lush and full of promise still ahead, and off we marched to pass through the portal which opened just enough to let us in and then sealed up behind us with a great whooshing sound, leaving the two of us blind as moles to fumble our way on a steep flight of stairs that wound tight and deep toward the center of we still don't know what.

I'm not going to say our eyes adjusted because what light was there for them to adjust to, any more than we adjusted to the fading smell of earth—which, sure, we were going to miss—but whether the stairs led up or down, we stumbled along them as best we could, the passage so narrow we had to turn sideways to shove our way through: down, down. Or else, up, up. We did this for a long time until, at last, they ended, delivering us into a great round room that looked, from the inside, exactly like the outside of the structure except with a kind of radiance seeping through the slats now warm and soft enough to drink and, at the very center, a nest of pillows big enough for two.

So here's what we did: You wrapped your arms around me, and I wrapped my arms around you, and we both fell down in a heap to sleep the sleep of the righteous dead, which who knows, maybe we were.

No one would ever believe what happened next.

After we sleep the sleep of the dead, we wake up to a swelling sound like a kind of breath or bloodbeat of the universe itself, and wouldn't you know it, but here we are off on a cruise of our own!

Ha!

But how do you drive a ship like this? And will there be dinner in it?

I'm a little bit cold, and you're a little bit hot, and we're both a little bit lonely, so we get up to explore, and the first thing we find is a hallway with doors that lead somewhere else, which now that we've left time behind us, we're in no hurry to find out. If we're in a rush for anything, it's to see where this hallway leads. You're hoping for a control room with instrument panels for lift and thrust and manuals for getting from here to there and a great bank of windows to see where we're going, and I'm hoping for a dining room with a table big enough for all of us.

But no, the only place the hallway leads is to the wall at the end of the world with a single portal in it so small we have to take turns peering out not at where we are headed but where we have been. So that's how we finally know for sure that it really is Earth where we lived through the interregnum, said goodbye to our parents, and lost our two boys. We know this because there it is behind us, every bit as round and blue as it once was in our memories of TV or the Internet, but with maybe a little less sparkle.

Don't worry, I tell you, because you will, but we both know it's only a matter of time before, absent of us, it will be sparkling all over again. That is the first thought that comes into our heads to fill up the blank part at the center of our brains which, now that we're sailing away is suddenly not so blank anymore, for the farther the planet falls away behind us, the more possible it is to conceive of everything we are leaving behind, all we've abandoned it to.

Don't get me wrong—I'm not making any kind of judgment here. We did what we did. It wasn't right or wrong. It just wasn't enough.

There were boys after all, and then they grew up. What else would boys do? They went through their stages—from small and sweet, to mopey and distant, to big and gone—all the while the one and constant center of our hearts until they marched off into the maw of the interregnum as if they could do one single thing about it. They took their phones, of course they did, small rectangular bulges in their back pockets, with buds in their ears. For a while we heard what we heard but then, one day, just nothing, our own phones as dead and as dark as night minus moon. Who confused our brains like this? Was it something in the water, or a chip? A special kind of ray? Nanobots blasted through our phones? When all we ever wanted was a word—one each from each boy, a single text is all—to let us know they were okay.

Unless, of course, they were not.

Maybe they turned into bankers instead! Do bankers text parents?

Now look at us like the thieves we are, stealing away in the night when the one thing we could have used now is a martini.

All that is left for us to do is think our thoughts and feel our rue as the holes in our brains knit themselves up now that it's far too late. Nothing to do, nothing to do but trade off at the portal and peer back through time, the layers and layers of it that accrue as you pass through your life. Peel back far enough and you're cradling the infant who cleaved you in two. Or further, and there's your mother cradling *you*, her arms strong and supple, not wizened at all. Somewhere inside us, these secret beings nest, but on the outside, not even a trace.

You peer through the portal and here's what you see: a boy with a board book running up to you like you are the greatest magician in the world because you can read it to him.

I see big and gawky teens with pimples on their faces and a sad forlornness to them hunkered over empty bowls so bleary-eyed from sleep they can't quite tell they're on their own. Where's my cereal? they whine. Who, now, will pour their cereal for them?

They're not always so cute, you say.

Don't think it won't happen to you, our parents chortled. No one escapes.

But *oh*! we are going to miss it, that planet that had once been lovely and ours for as long as we walked on its surface, but not as much as we miss the boys who disappeared somewhere between men in the prime of their life and what the interregnum held in store for all of us. I'd wanted a different kind of ending, one with a little open destiny of hope. They deserved that much—all children do. Or at least another planet of their own where everything is nice.

Goodbye water planet, we cry.

But goodbye, too, to the interregnum, which we're not sorry to leave! Hurrah!

Goodbye, goodbye, goodbye.

Goodbye to our parents, who grew old and hoary.

Goodbye to our sons, who did not.

And as soon as we think that something breaks open in us. I'm not going to call it love, but why not? Love for our parents, who loved us first, love for our boys we loved best, love for the planet we've abandoned them to, love for the ship we're sailing away on, love for you, love for me. Any way you look at it, we are the lucky ones. We had it all. Don't ask us why. We don't know what happened to our sons after their phones went dead, but boys love their mothers. We know that much.

At least that's what we tell ourselves as we let our minds drift toward the sadness of sleep. Something is still going to happen, and we guess we'll find out when we get there. If I could fire up my phone and send a message back to Earth, what should it say, I wonder—brush your teeth, take care of your brother, good luck?

I'll tell you what it wouldn't say. It wouldn't say, say, *ta-ta.* It wouldn't say, wish you were here.

So this is how it happens that we find ourselves zipping through all outer space on the one escapeship that ever came for anyone, with our dear, doomed planet spinning away behind us until it's just another star and our hearts as broken as ever, when suddenly I hear a *beep*!

Visitation

We knew something was going to happen. We just didn't know what. The signs were everywhere.

In the crepuscular hours of dawn and dusk, animals we didn't recognize came out of the hills. They made harsh, sawing brays or mournful hoots and were misshapen, although neither of us could say what their proper form might be. You said they were searching for water.

I said, why don't they have hair.

Fur, you said, because you always like to correct me.

Every morning we'd awaken to a persistent low-grade dread, our heads all fat and furry with the stale aftermath of dreams we wished we could forget. On the inside, a kind of festering, we were burning up. But on the outside, well, you know how it was. You, yelling at every little thing; me, sobbing at nothing.

After our parents were gone, the neighbors had not been far behind, some dashing out in broad daylight to jump in the cars that still came for them, loaded with luggage and gear. But most left first thing in the morning, trudging down the road that led to the flats where who knew what was happening now? They were carrying stuff they were going to need in overstuffed backpacks with tubes to drink through. They held hands with their kids. On their feet were the ruggedest shoes they owned; on their heads, caps with team logos or floppy-brimmed bonnets. I don't know why we missed the boat.

Boat, you say, don't say boat!

I don't like it when you use that tone with me, but most of the time I deserve it. People went where they went. And if we hadn't been left behind like stunned birds on the ground from the soft, missing part of our brains, we might have gone too.

It was a long time already since any bird had flown into our window.

Later, you come back from the market, but the tuna is gone, you complain, there hasn't been frisée in months, and someone—you're not saying who—bought up all the gin and vodka as if for a cruise.

In other respects, the quiet was nice. We could be inside it and think all the thoughts we had, which, to be fair, were not very many. Sometimes, while you were busy napping on the couch, I closed my eyes and tried to think of things like children on park swings or hunched over school desks doing sums or writing ditties for their mothers. But we mainly just sat around with our doldrums and deplored the disappearing chunks of our brains, the high, thin voice, or maybe two, that called to us in our dreams—*I'm falling*. But where was there to fall?

Other than that, pretty much nothing.

The end.

But no, not yet.

One day a knock came to our door.

Then a quiet shuffling, a sound like a mew.

Mewl, you said, because you always like to have the last word.

But that's not what I meant.

We hadn't had a package in months and the only remaining people we knew were off snorkeling somewhere in Earth's last coral reefs. But *oh*! maybe it was someone else, someone we did know—no, *loved*—come back to save us! Then we both sighed the same sigh at once. If it were someone like that, they'd be barging in without knocking at all. So who could it be?

No good, you said because you like to be a know-it-all, can come from a muffled knock, but since I had to agree, we decided to ignore it.

Then the knock came again, more a little tap and with something furtive to it.

I sighed.

You sighed.

We glanced at each other, uncertain what to do. You were sitting on the sofa, the color of brick; I was sitting on the chair, the color of chartreuse, but not even in the interregnum could we sit on them forever.

Okay you said at last, I'll go.

Okay, I said with some relief, you go. But wear a mask.

Your feet on the stairs were as heavy as my heart. If I slipped out the back, I might be able to bushwhack it up to the store on my own. We used to be more generous than this, I didn't even have time to think because the next thing I heard from the bottom of the stairs sounded like nothing I'd heard for so long I couldn't quite parse it at first.

Oh-ho, you said. What do we have here?

You said it as if speaking from another century or planet, with something so strange in your voice I had to go peer from the top of the stairs, and this made my breath go down to a place so deep in my lungs that I couldn't quite breathe it all out at first.

It was small, what you had, half again the size of us, or even of our parents, who'd been shrinking. I didn't quite know how to think this, but it seemed what you had was a child. What wasn't clear, from where I stood, was if it was a boy or a girl, or when it had last eaten, or even what color it was under all that dirt.

I was still at the top of the stairs, and you were still at the bottom near the door, keeping the either boy or girl on the outside, but with nothing you could do about the smell. You weren't really barring its entry, but you weren't all *mi casa es su casa* either. You were prudent as was proper and your wont.

Oh-ho, you said again, as if you didn't know what else to say. Who would?

Mewl, the sound came back. Or was that a little hiccough at the end?

It had been so long since we had seen a child—any kind of child, dirty or clean—we didn't know what to do. Even the word for such a small being—for *child*—felt strange in our heads, although we couldn't have said why that might be: Would it stir something up? Did it hurt?

So you said it a third time. You said, *oh-ho!*

And I said—I don't quite know why, the words just flew out of my mouth—for Christ's sake, throw a bucket of water on it and see what comes out. Of all the words I said, the word Christ surprised me the most. I never used to talk like that, I know.

After the water, a girl came out, or what passed for a girl.

Now soap, I directed from the top of the stairs. Use the scrubber. Does she have teeth?

It turned out the girl did have some teeth but whether the milk ones had fallen out and the soft child gums were still waiting for the permanents to come in, or if there was something wrong with the permanents and they weren't ever coming in, or if the permanents had come in already and then fallen out again, it was hard to tell, for like the color of the skin, so, too, the age of the child: to wit, completely indeterminate. A child as old as time itself we didn't yet know how to think.

You kept her down there a good long while, scrubbing with a loofah and what passed for soap in what used to be our carport, and when you were done, you shook the water off, wrapped her in one of your t-shirts that fell to her calves and slipped from her shoulder like a sexy negligee, and brought her upstairs to me. And that was that. She had a little tummy and a bunch of bony limbs and a big head on a skinny neck, but all in all, she seemed okay.

Why hello, I said with what I meant as my nicest smile, even if it felt like a grimace.

And she said what she said. She said, mewl.

You hadn't done a thing to get the knots out of her hair, which turned out to be a bright coppery color that made me want to touch it, just run my fingers through it like a pelt or mane, but as soon I lifted my hand, the girl pulled away with an inauspicious jerk. That, the recoil, told us something. It told us a lot.

We knew we had to feed her, but feed her exactly what?

I know! you said. How about an egg?

But you knew and I knew we had only the one egg. We'd had the one egg for a while. You wanted to save it for a special occasion, and I wanted to save it for a hundred years or an emergency—one egg as a hedge against or vindication of the future. But which was this?

I think, I said, we have a cracker. Would a cracker do?

In the larder, we also had an onion, a tin of fish, and a bag of donut holes, the sugarless kind. What good was a sugarless donut, you said, much less the hole, but I liked the way you could pop in in it in your mouth and hold it open in a round and joyous "O." Outside where we'd planted a few things on the hill, we also had some carrots and a beanstalk and something green and leafy that gave me indigestion and you gas.

Then the girl mewled again, the sound coming out like a thing that could curl around my heart and squeeze such that all I wanted was to pull her close and hug her and hug her until there wasn't anything more she was ever going to need in the world. That's what I wanted. I wanted it as if there was another thing inside me or a missing thing I needed to fill up. But whenever I tried to touch her, the same little jerk—more like a flinch. So what was wrong with me that she had to do that when a short bit ago she'd stood docilely mewling while you doused her with water and scrubbed her with what passed for soap?

That's when I decided: She could have the egg if she let me touch her, or her me. It wouldn't have to be a cuddle, although a cuddle would be nice. Just, if she would tug a little at my pinkie or poke me on the hip or let me pat her on the head or pull her on my lap. I know how this makes me sound, but fair was fair. Once we made contact, I would be in her court for ever and ever, but until then, not even a stale old sugarless donut hole for her. After, didn't I have a little packet of sweetener somewhere I could break out for a special treat?

Some things hurt more than others, then and now. You said give her time, don't be all grabby. Think of everything she's been through.

But hadn't we been through a lot too?

Just because she was small didn't mean things were harder for her, but I knew I was wrong. Children don't pop up out of nowhere. They come from somewhere. In the somewhere—the *home*—a mother and/or father, a brother/sister, a cuddle thing, a toothbrush, a nana. At night, they drift through dreamy dreams or lie awake with gloomy dread. Their little clothes lie in a heap on the floor. They smell of something barely human. And, relentlessly, they grow—from fresh and tiny, to in-between, to one day being fully set like you and me—but with the world coming at them the whole time, inexorable and utterly opaque: What if something happens to their parents? Why do they have to go to school, and later, why not? What's for dinner—why isn't there ever anything to eat?

The next thing you said brought tears to my eyes. You said, but really, doesn't she remind you of someone?

And that was that because right away when you said that, the girl buried her face in my belly and started to cry, from mewl to whimper, like something being pulled from inside her to the outside, which pretty soon tears were rolling down my face too—her tears, my tears, all the tears left in the world—until even you were crying, and we were all huddled all together, her on my lap and me in yours and our arms around each other until we were done and I broke out those old donut holes and found that packet of sweetener and we had a little feast. Then the girl curled up into the little nest of pillows you made for her on the floor to sleep like it really was the end of the world.

Here's what happened next: We went downstairs to bed.

And when we woke up in the morning, you said what a dream you had had, and I did too, but when we went up for our memory of coffee, there she was still, a little rumpled heap of hair and mewl.

After that, we settled into a kind of routine: Weep, eat, cuddle, sleep.

Sleep, eat, weep, cuddle.

Weep.

Sleep.

Eat.

Cuddle.

Sleep.

You liked to say she was cute as a button, although in truth, she was not. Neither was she pretty as a picture nor neat as a pin. She was a scrawny little thing with a pointy nose and chin, and no matter what we did, she would not stop mewling. Still, nothing was broken that we could tell. Her eyes were clear, her teeth—the ones she had—firmly attached in her little mouth, and her new clean smell was fine, a bit earthy, like you.

Mewl, she said, mewl.

I know, you said, why not slip a little whiskey in her milk?

But where would we get the milk? And what whiskey?

As soon as I said that a sudden skulk came over you, as if you were hiding something from me, something important, something like whiskey. We'd eaten all the donut holes by now and wolfed down the cracker, but if you had a secret stash of whiskey, I had a hoard of beans. Did little girls like beans? Yes! And she liked stewed tomatoes. She even liked canned okra and asparagus and peas. She liked everything in every can I had but not your whiskey. When you gave her whiskey, she made a face and spat it back at you.

This went on for a while, and as long as it lasted, we went on as before, reading our books and mourning our TV, pruning our plants and nursing our regret, but even if the smell of the girl in lieu of the smell that was missing in my brain or the feel of her body in my erstwhile empty lap were familiar, if not quite familiar enough, there was nothing we could do about it now.

And it couldn't last forever.

When it was just you and me, we did okay. I hardly ate anything and neither did you. Now, with the girl, things were different. She was small, but she was hungry, and despite how I dissembled about the larder to begin with, the cans and legumes were finite, and we were too. But when I marched you to the larder to prove my point, you just sidled up beside me and slipped your hand in mine as in a kind of prayer.

Oh look, you said slyly, surveying our few remaining cans, peaches!

That night I woke up with a feeling in the blank part of my brain, a swelled up feeling like the answer to a puzzle in a dream where everyone else knows what it is, only not you. You're completely in the dark.

I lay there for a while, thinking my thoughts. I thought about you, and I thought about the girl. I thought about our parents, and I thought about the photo they had sent us from their cruise: our moms suited up in snorkeling gear and our dads in sporty aloha shirts, all four of them waving their wizened arms like life's a lark, what's wrong with you? Then I did the thing with my breath, the in and the out. If it came to a choice between me or a cruise, which would you choose? This got me pitching, though, because you can't pretend a cane is a stick forever and maybe you were right that the people who looked like our parents were really alien imposters dropped here from outer space to confuse what was left of our brains.

So who really took our sticks—intruders? children who used them to trek down the hill away from us and meant to return them one day?

Boys!

I remembered that now.

Boys! *Boys!*

Two fierce and beautiful, ornery boys, stubborn as stones and fine as wheat, with coal dark eyes and enormous hearts, more than enough for both of us, too much. I can't remember anything else—did they squabble? were they neat or messy, picky eaters or robust? I know they did not mind—children never do. They are lying little cheats with snotty snouts and stubs for toes, which is why God made them so adorable and helpless. Well, not God per se, but you know what I mean. Of course, they squabbled— they were children. *Boys!* And *oh!* they started out so very, very small. Sometimes, it hurt to look at them, they were so small. How could such small things endure in this wearying time we had already entered long before now?

Some will and some won't, you said.

And of course, you were right.

One of the children had dark hair and the other, light. They came that way from the start, I remembered that too and for a moment—that moment—felt a bit of clarity, if not peace. We had a house with children in it. We did everything we could to keep them safe and teach them things like how to read and throw a ball. We loved them so!

But then, I don't know—I'd lost something. There was a child on my hip—a small child—and another slightly bigger one running around the house—not our sweet little house in the hills but another house—a house in the flats— where there once were boys. And I was chasing him, this slightly bigger boy because we had somewhere to be and why would he run away like that at such a time? I know! I was looking for his shoe. It was time to take them somewhere. I had to take them to the doctor—a pediatrician—a doctor for children, I mean. One of the children—the one on my hip—was wearing two shoes, but the other—the one I was chasing—just one.

We didn't know yet what was coming, not even an inkling. We turned on the lights when it got dark. We had coffee every morning, with milk and any amount of fat we wanted in it. The boys were always bickering—over what, baseball cards, joysticks, TV? This was the way it had always been but not for long. Surely, we should have noticed something, the signs were everywhere—new shoes every few months, a refrigerator crammed with food, the silence that came down on us all when the moody moods rose up.

At last, the little one, in my arms, burst out, *tee-hee*— it's in the hamper.

What's in the hamper?

The shoe, he cried with glee, that's where I put my brother's shoe. I hid it from you!

We told you, we told you, our parents crowed. *Ta-ta,* their postcard said. Think of everything we did for you, it didn't have to say.

Who loses track of children anyway?

Well, except us.

Did our parents take them on their cruise, did they march off with our hiking sticks, were they abducted by a spaceship or just trying to get home when something happened, could we have been so unlucky as all that?

Something froze up in our hearts then. It froze up good. If there was anything left to feel, we didn't know what it was, what with boys disappearing into the interregnum and hoary old people getting everything they wanted—martinis, hiking sticks, a luxury cruise on a finite planet at the end of time. You said it first: Things seem the same, but trust me, they are not. Because what they don't have on this planet is what's missing from the blank parts of our brains, which when I finally sort it out, I sit up gasping from the bed.

And then I think my final thought, because sometimes things sneak up on you in the night like that: *If there were children, where are they now?*

In the morning, when we go upstairs, there she is, already awake and making our coffee—one cup for you, one cup for me.

Then she does something that surprises us even more. She says, cream?

It's a word—her first—but that's not why we're gaping. We're gaping because where did she get the cream? And now all at once, she can't stop jabbering, this once mewling mute of a girl, spinning words out from that one word "cream," some recognizable—"nacre," "peril," "stone," "ineffable"—others not, hopping all the while up and down, first on one foot, then the other (how does she *do* that?) as if trying to tell us something—something *important*.

Didn't we used to have a French dictionary? you say.

That's not French, I say.

What it is, is hard to say. It doesn't sound like any language we have heard before, or rather, it sounds like all the languages jumbled together as if full of promises no one can keep. It's nice to have cream for our coffee, but a little peace and quiet would be nice too.

Lapth gablot wrktl, the girl says.

And this goes on all day.

By the time we are lying side-by-side in our bed, the night sky outside down to the color of nothing, my ears are ringing and yours are too. So we turn on the white noise and roll back-to-back on our sides, neither one of us wanting to go to sleep yet because lately our dreams have been getting mixed up, as if we're both dreaming the same dream but never at once. You awake with relics of mine on your tongue while I'm always just catching up. But we don't really want to stay awake either because, what for? We do this every night. But the girl has not stopped talking all day, and after the bucket and what passed for soap, what more could she want? What more could we do?

Then you are the one to start talking for no reason on earth, launching in on another of your theories, like whatever made us think we should keep her in the first place when shouldn't we really have marched her off down to the flats like anyone else, put a tag on her that said *did you lose this child* or *found*! But no, not us. Did we ever once consider another couple somewhere out there with a blank spot in the center of their brains where their child used to be? And if no one claimed her, we could have sent her to our parents. The cruises weren't for children, but what could they have done if we shipped her in a box? One of the grandmas could have taught her to swim, the other, a little algebra and history. A musical instrument would have been nice, one you could blow on or pluck with your fingers.

Before long you have talked us both into a twisted-up knot of despair, but then, right on the dreaded cusp of sleep, it turns out you're not done. You have more.

What I mean, you conclude, a bit smug, is we have to take her back.

Wait, what—back where?

Then, because neither one of us wants to think about that, we go to sleep.

And this was the loneliest feeling of all because I'm about to have my own dream for once in which the sky is full of spaceships and exploding things, and I'm squatting by a river with two boys and a fish. It's a fat fish, like a blowfish, and I'm splitting it down its spine and smoothing its two sides open in soft hairy flaps as I tell the two boys to be patient, I must do this for them. On the other side of the river, a woman is running toward something, but why is she doing that? Not now, I think, not yet. I think I love this woman. I know I want her to be safe, but now I see that it's a child she's running toward—a *young* child, a toddler. She's rushing toward the toddler but can only get so close before one of the exploding things goes off above them. Here's how close she gets: Her skin peels off her face and there's a wall of flames between them now, but she can still hear the child shrieking. I can hear it too—that baby is hysterical—so I turn to the boys to placate them with fish, but they're gone, and the fish is gone too. All that is left in the world is me on my side of the river and the screams of the child on the other side and a voice in my head saying that even though I don't know what has happened—what terrible calamity has occasioned this—it's only a matter of time before I am the one rushing into the maelstrom to save a person I love.

And when I wake up, it is already here.

Okay I say, if you insist. But let's not go today. Let's go tomorrow.

Interregnum

I didn't know what to call it, and you didn't either. If we had to call it anything, we might have said delirium, or spell—a spell come over us. It was a dark time in the history of the world.

Or universe. You could say universe. Things were that grim.

First, the delirium. Then, the interregnum. We argued for a while about lower case or upper but finally settled on the article as a kind of compromise, as if that might contain things or guarantee an after.

The middle comes after the beginning, we said, and after that, the end! Ha!

We were living in a house then, a sweet little house in the hills with a back wall of glass that looked out on the hills and all that was left of the world. It wasn't a lot, but it wasn't nothing either. We had a nearby market where you could buy milk and frisée, when there was frisée, a fireplace that all you had to do was turn the key and light the flame, pots and pans. Maybe we lacked what we used to call a purpose, but we had parents—and footwear. I had a whole pile of shoes, and you had a mountain of socks, but despite this certain bounty, we still took our shoes off before coming upstairs to the room filled with light where we lived by day until going back down to sleep at night. Upstairs, socks; downstairs, sleep.

No one wanted things to happen the way they did.

We called it a disaster, but it was worse than that.

Everyone, right at the first, was full of ideas for how to change things back.

But nothing we did made any difference.

We all felt so helpless.

After a while, it began to seem as if this was the way it had been, just you and me in that sweet little house looking out at the way things used to be. I mean, the hill with its grass and scrubby chaparral, the great dead oak, the rocks that sometimes worked their way up out of the ground from a riverbed so ancient just thinking of that— its ancientness—gave us a feeling both beautiful and sad. Sometimes, small flowers popped out of the ground, but they didn't last long, dug up in the night by whatever it is that digs such things up.

What else?

One time, a bird flew into our window. It hit with a sudden thud and fell stunned to the ground. Neither of us wanted to touch it. Aren't birds dirty? Don't they carry disease? So we left it where it was and after a while, it flew away. And that's what the interregnum was like, but with us lying stunned on the ground.

Sometimes, even breathing felt hard.

What else?

You had a mother and a father, and I did too, hoary old people bent over and slow, with whiskers on their chins and strings of whatever they were eating in their teeth. Our parents welcomed the interregnum. Praise be, they would have said if they said words like that. Despite our disaster, they were *happy* about it. Whereas, for us, a terrible keeling.

Our parents were very old, so their thinking about such things was in the decline, but once they saw what was happening on the other channel, no argument on earth could make them switch it back. Sharing genes, we had the same kinds of faces, but on the inside, what had happened to our parents? Weren't they the ones who taught us always to try to live in the right? Still, they liked to drink martinis, and we did too, so that's what we did to smooth over our differences vis-à-vis the spell we'd fallen under—the one our parents welcomed and that left us like birds on the ground.

I breathe in.

You breathe out.

Your bird had brown feet with yellow markings; mine, marbled the color of blood. This is how we remembered things—pretty much the same, a little bit different.

Our parents liked their martinis with gin, we liked ours with vodka, otherwise, pretty much the same.

But don't you remember how they started out, normal old people bent over and slow with their three-footed canes, when wham, the two worlds—their world, our world—collided. This pepped them up somehow, it pepped them up a lot. Here's how much it pepped them up: Our hiking sticks went missing. That's odd, we thought, didn't we just have them out on a stroll, when *lah dee dah*, here come our parents, swinging sticks that look a lot like ours.

Still, stuff was going on. Gin, vodka: unbelievable. You knew it and I knew it, but neither one of us wanted to say anything. Why stir things up when things were plenty stirred up as it was? There we sat at the dinner table, slumped where they were straight, ashen where they were ruddy, although that could have been the gin. And somewhere between us, blank spaces with no one in them gave us a feeling we didn't know what.

But yet they were our parents, so we loved them. Let them have their last hurrah.

Hurrah! Hurrah!

No one knew when the delirium started, it was just a sign of worse to come. How could we know the future? There was no rain. The hills dried up. The light turned sharp and brittle, like a glare. Whereas elsewhere, the rain wouldn't stop—buckets and buckets a day—causing the rivers to rise, the dams to break.

Didn't I say this was going to happen? you say.

I say, in the market we had blackberries and artichokes, frisée. We had wine.

Just wait, you say, things will get better.

Harrumph, I say, they could get worse.

The house we lived in wasn't that big, but it wasn't that small either. It had room enough for us. It had room for more.

What else did it have? A file for bills, soft rugs for our feet, powerpacks, tchotchkes and doodads and windows galore. Who wants a house with so many windows?

But after a while, you got used to the light.

You always said it started with the bird, but in my heart, I trace it back much further. At first, we didn't want to talk about it. After that, we forgot.

We were forgetting so much, one thing and another disappearing from our brains.

Forgetting made things easier somehow.

But it also made them harder, our heads drifting down to our hands in our most familiar posture of despair.

Sometimes, at night, in the sweet, sad hour before sleep, we talked about how nice it would be to be under the ground already: hurry up, hurry up. No boxes for us, just our not-yet-so-very-old-bodies covered with dirt for the worms to eat all the way down to our boney-bone bones, the green to replace us above.

Oh you, our parents said, we've seen it all already. What made you think you were so special it wouldn't ever happen to you?

Then our mothers said, as they often did, think of someone other than yourselves.

We woke up every day, and—just *nothing*. The house was there, the day outside, the hours.

In our pockets, we carried our phones, as if we could still fire them up to small beloved faces beaming back at us from inside them like relics. We could fire them up, all right, but the faces in them weren't anything familiar but strangers with shadows of beards on muscular chins, squinted eyes, a bit of a droop. The feeling those faces gave us was not happiness or love, but more like someone came in the night and clipped a chunk out of our brain. Sometimes, my thoughts would go straight to this spot where nothing was like a tongue to the hole where a tooth used to be.

We told you, we told you, our parents crowed, this is the way things are meant to be!

We don't agree on this—we don't agree on anything. But they still text us on our phones and show up every night, twirling our old sticks and poking us with them if we are slow to get them their martinis. Then we give them something from the market for their dinner. We sit at the table like always, except older, and with something missing from it. They look all right, our parents, a lot like they used to. Brighter, maybe, with shinier teeth. If I cover my ears, I won't have to hear the words that come out of their mouths.

Eat your vegetables, they used to say, but that won't help us now, because even though they are our parents and we love them, we know who brought the interregnum down on all of us.

One night, after we've had our martinis and given our parents something to eat and sent them off toddling to wherever they sleep at night, which, don't get me started, is not going to be here, you tell me a story.

It begins, you begin, with the end of the world as we know it.

We're either upstairs on the sofa waiting for the moon to fill up the big windows or downstairs in the quiet zone of darkness of our bed waiting for sleep, but either way, I nod and cozy up to you, nuzzling my head into your gentle mound of chest because, well, who doesn't like stories. I'm listening. I'm thinking, okay, world's done, what next?

But not, you go on, as we most vividly imagined it.

What, I say. No nuclear winter? No giant meteors or zombie plagues?

No, you tell me gently, and there's a kindness to you I have missed, just secret transpositions imposed on us in the night when no one is watching. Whereas by day, what can I say? If someone gives you grits for breakfast, they can make you think it is an Egg McMuffin! Some people start building bunkers in the ground and stocking up on honey while others pretend nothing has changed, including having progeny and nest eggs. And even if a bunch of them don colorful hats and march in the streets, nothing they do makes any difference.

Then stuff started happening, you said.

It was probably always happening crosstown or a couple of blocks over, say, and as long as things stayed where they were, you could go ahead and have your *grande latte* or your *lah-de-dah*. But when the interregnum came to our front door, hunkered down and wouldn't budge, the stuff I am talking about, you can't even believe. And it ends—it always ends—with violence.

Maybe, I sniff, some people were watching, just not the right people—not *us*.

But no, you insist, that's how the interregnum works. One day, we wake up and there's another world in place of the one we went to sleep in the night before. There's a kind of déjà vu to it, as if this happens all the time. We look around for the spaceship that abducted us to this strange new planet where everything seems the same but isn't or else whisked all the others away and left deep-fake imposters in their place. But something's wrong and something's missing, something important we can't quite remember, something we love. We promise to be good—to eat our peas and water our few remaining trees—if only we can get back the blank part of our brains, but it's no use. A spaceship came. The transposition is complete.

You never used to be so gloomy, so I push back a bit. What do you mean, *we*? Maybe *you* slipped a quark or two over into a parallel universe. Maybe you'll slip back tomorrow, right as rain!

No, you insist, it's bigger than quarks.

I think about that for a minute, and then it hits me. You don't mean *everyone*! Not our parents—not our mothers and fathers!

Especially our mothers and fathers, you say. And then you say, the end.

Wait, what, I say? You can't just say the end.

Here, though, is some proof you might offer.

Some nights the moon disappeared from our sky.

The children craved sweet things for breakfast.

One of my teeth ached. Only the one.

Unpleasant odors wafted from unpleasant things.

Glass broke when it was thrown in the street.

I'm thinking interregnum is too good a word for what was happening to us now. What more is there to say? Things were one way, then they were another, and even though it seemed to happen overnight, it took longer than that, a few months at least.

Here's what I missed: our mothers' gentle faces, the way they had with flowers, something else.

Here's what I wanted: to stuff a sock in our fathers' faces and shut up their gloating.

We're breathing together and hoping as hard as we can for something not this, but the blank part in our brains keeps getting bigger and even though we know that, even deep inside the interregnum, love between a parent and a child remains a precious thing, no matter how many stories we tell or quarrels we quell, a time is coming sooner and sooner when everyone is going to swig one too many martinis, and once we start in on all the reasons they are wrong and we are right—*yah!*—there will never be a way to stop what happens next.

After the yelling, the quiet was worse.

All the next day, we waited for the cocktail hour so someone—any of us—could say that we were sorry. I would have said it. You would have said it. But no one showed up for martinis, not that night, not ever again.

By the end of the week, they'd gone off on a cruise.

Bon voyage, read the words that pop up on our phones, even though they were the ones who were leaving.

Here's what they don't say: *x o x o x o.*

Ta-ta, they say.

But what? No wait. You can't just go like that. Despite our disagreements, oh please, not now. Not yet.

Of all times to go off on a cruise, right at the height of the interregnum. And really, at *their* age, we think.

But we don't really mean it.

Here's what we really mean: Well, here we are, two hapless orphans all alone on the planet. *Now what are we going to do?*

Acknowledgments

Some of these accounts appeared in a chapbook, *Assumptions We Might Make About the Postworld,* Ricochet Editions (2018).

The following accounts first appeared as below:

Account P, as "The Gift of Common Memory," in "Diptych: Girl, Memory," *LitroNY* (Spring 2020).

Account B, as "The Bunch" in "Diptych: Bunch, Duck/Dog," *Fairy Tale Review* (Spring 2019, online).

Account A, as "Teeth," Account G2 as "Dreambreath," and Account T as "Us-vs-Them," as "Triptych: Teeth, Dreambreath, Us-vs-Them," *Fiction International* (Fall 2018).

Account M, as "Call It Milk," *Barrelhouse* (Summer 2018).

Account F as "A Flower of Its Own" and Account R as "Each One, One," as "Diptych: Flower, One," *Lumina* (Spring 2018).

Account K as "The Heaviness of Lead" and Account G as "The Master of Goats," as "Diptych: Lead, Goats," *december* (Spring 2017).

Account F3 as "A Crown of Gold Fuzz," *Litro* 2016.

Account F2 as "A Festival of Fish," Account S as "Not Here," Account P2 as "How We Started" and Account P4 as "Assumptions We Might Make About the Postworld," in "Quartet: Sometime After That," *Chicago Quarterly Review* (Fall 2016). "Assumptions We Might Make About the Postworld" also appears in the COLA 25 Artist's catalog.

Account N as "It Being Forbidden" and Account C as "Like a Red Rubber Ball, as "Diptych: Forbidden, Red Rubber Ball," *Shenandoah* (Spring 2016).

Account E as "Television News," *West Branch* (Spring 2016, online).

Account A as "The Hunger of Aliens," *The Sonora Review*, 58 (Fall 2010).

The author wishes to thank the Djerassi Artist's Residence Program and Leonardo/Scientific Delirium Madness; the Virginia Center for the Creative Arts; and California State University, Northridge, for their support. Also, Rod, Mona, Annette, for their generous reading and enduring friendship. And Lisa, for all the art.

Katharine Haake is the author of the eco-dystopian science fiction fable, *The Time of Quarantine*; the California hybrid prose lyric, *That Water, Those Rocks*; and three collections of stories. Her work has appeared broadly and been recognized as distinguished by *Best American Fiction* and *Best American Essays*, among others. She is a professor emerita at California State University, Northridge, and lives in Los Angeles.

11:11 Press is an American independent literary publisher based in Minneapolis, MN. Founded in 2018, 11:11 publishes innovative literature of all forms and varieties. We believe in the freedom of artistic expression, the realization of creative potential, and the transcendental power of stories.

www.ingramcontent.com/pod-product-compliance
Lightning Source LLC
Chambersburg PA
CBHW020821190726
48285CB00006B/2363